PRAISE FOR

MW01074047

"In Robinson's latest ac ... ..., jack Sigler, King of the Chess Team--a Delta Forces unit whose gonzo members take the names of chess pieces--tackles his most harrowing mission yet.Threshold elevates Robinson to the highest tier of over-the-top action authors and it delivers beyond the expectations even of his fans. The next Chess Team adventure cannot come fast enough."-- **Booklist - Starred Review**

"In Robinson's wildly inventive third Chess Team adventure (after Instinct), the U.S. president, Tom Duncan, joins the team in mortal combat against an unlikely but irresistible gang of enemies, including "regenerating capybara, Hydras, Neander-thals, [and] giant rock monsters." ...Video game on a page? Absolutely. Fast, furious unabashed fun? You bet." -- **Publishers Weekly**

"Jeremy Robinson's *Threshold* is one hell of a thriller, wildly imaginative and diabolical, which combines ancient legends and modern science into a non-stop action ride that will keep you turning the pages until the wee hours. Relentlessly gripping from start to finish, don't turn your back on this book!" -- **Douglas Preston, New York Times bestselling author of Impact and Blasphemy**

"With *Threshold* Jeremy Robinson goes pedal to the metal into very dark territory. Fast-paced, action-packed and wonderfully creepy! Highly recommended!" -- **Jonathan Maberry, *New York Times* bestselling author of *The King of Plagues* and *Rot & Ruin***

"*Threshold* is a blisteringly original tale that blends the thriller and horror genres in a smooth and satisfying hybrid mix. With his new entry in the Jack Sigler series, Jeremy Robinson plants his feet firmly on territory blazed by David Morrell and James Rollins. The perfect blend of mysticism and monsters, both human and otherwise, make *Threshold* as groundbreaking as it is riveting." -- **Jon Land,** *New York Times* **bestselling author of** *Strong Enough to Die*

"Jeremy Robinson is the next James Rollins."-- **Chris Kuzneski, New York Times bestselling author of The Lost Throne and The Prophecy**

"Jeremy Robinson's *Threshold* sets a blistering pace from the very first page and never lets up. This globe-trotting thrill ride challenges its well-crafted heroes with ancient mysteries, fantastic creatures, and epic action sequences. For readers seeking a fun rip-roaring adventure, look no further."
 -- **Boyd Morrison, bestselling author of** *The Ark*

"Robinson artfully weaves the modern day military with ancient history like no one else."-- **Dead Robot Society**

"THRESHOLD is absolutely gripping. A truly unique story mixed in with creatures and legendary figures of mythology, technology and more fast-paced action than a Jerry Bruckheimer movie. If you want fast-paced: you got it. If you want action: you got it. If you want mystery: you got it, and if you want intrigue, well, you get the idea. In short, I $@#!$% loved this one."-- **thenovelblog.com**

"As always the Chess Team is over the top of the stratosphere, but anyone who relishes an action urban fantasy thriller that combines science and mythology will want to join them for the exhilarating Pulse pumping ride."-- **Genre Go Round Reviews**

INSTINCT

"If you like thrillers original, unpredictable and chock-full of action, you are going to love Jeremy Robinson's Chess Team. INSTINCT riveted me to my chair." -- **Stephen Coonts, NY Times bestselling author of THE DISCIPLE and DEEP BLACK: ARCTIC GOLD**

"Robinson's slam-bang second Chess Team thriller [is a] a wildly inventive yarn that reads as well on the page as it would play on a computer screen."-- **Publisher's Weekly**

"Intense and full of riveting plot twists, it is Robinson's best book yet, and it should secure a place for the Chess Team on the A-list of thriller fans who like the over-the-top style of James Rollins and Matthew Reilly." -- **Booklist**

"Jeremy Robinson is a fresh new face in adventure writing and will make a mark in suspense for years to come." -- **David Lynn Golemon, NY Times bestselling author of LEGEND and EVENT**

"Instinct is a jungle fever of raw adrenaline that goes straight for the jugular."-- **Thomas Greanias, NY Times bestselling author of THE ATLANTIS PROPHECY and THE PROMISED WAR**

PULSE

"Robinson's latest reads like a video game with tons of action and lots of carnage. The combination of mythology, technology, and high-octane action proves irresistible. Gruesome and nasty in a good way, this will appeal to readers of Matthew Reilly." -- **Booklist**

"Raiders of the Lost Arc meets Tom Clancy meets Saturday matinee monster flick with myths, monsters, special ops supermen and more high tech weapons than a Bond flick. Pulse is an over-the-top, bullet-ridden good time." -- **Scott Sigler, New York Times bestselling author of CONTAGIOUS and INFECTED**

"Jeremy Robinson's latest novel, PULSE, ratchets his writing to the next level. Rocket-boosted action, brilliant speculation, and the recreation of a horror out of the mythologic past, all seamlessly blend into a rollercoaster ride of suspense and adventure. Who knew chess could be this much fun!" -- **James Rollins, New York Times bestselling author of THE LAST ORACLE**

PULSE contains all of the danger, treachery, and action a reader could wish for. Its band of heroes are gutsy and gritty. Jeremy Robinson has one wild imagination, slicing and stitching his tale together with the deft hand of a surgeon. Robinson's impressive talent is on full display in this one." -- **Steve Berry, New York Times bestselling author of THE CHARLE-MAGNE PURSUIT**

" Jeremy Robinson dares to craft old-fashioned guilty pleasures - far horizons, ancient maps, and classic monsters - hardwired for the 21st century. There's nothing timid about Robinson as he drops his readers off the cliff without a parachute and somehow manages to catch us an inch or two from doom." -- **Jeff Long, New York Times bestselling author of THE DESCENT and YEAR ZERO**

CALLSIGN:

BISHOP

JEREMY ROBINSON

WITH DAVID McAFEE

BREAKNECK MEDIA

Visit Jeremy Robinson on the World Wide Web at:
 www.jeremyrobinsononline.com

Visit David McAfee on the World Wide Web at:
mcafeeland.wordpress.com

FICTION BY JEREMY ROBINSON

The Jack Sigler Thrillers
Threshold
Instinct
Pulse
Callsign: King - Book 1
Callsign: Queen - Book 1
Callsign: Rook - Book 1
Callsign: Bishop - Book 1
Callsign: Knight - Book 1
Callsign: King - Book 2 – Underworld

The Antarktos Saga
The Last Hunter – Descent
The Last Hunter – Pursuit
The Last Hunter - Ascent

Origins Editions (first five novels)
Kronos
Antarktos Rising
Beneath
Raising the Past
The Didymus Contingency

Writing as Jeremy Bishop
Torment
The Sentinel

Short Stories
Insomnia

Humor
The Zombie's Way (Ike Onsoomyu)
The Ninja's Path (Kutyuso Deep)

FICTION BY DAVID MCAFEE

Bachiyr Novels
33 A.D.
Saying Goodbye to the Sun
61 A.D.

Horror Novels
*NASTY LITTLE F!#*ERS*
The Gallows Tree (Coming Soon)

Short Story Collections
The Lake and 17 Other Stories
Devil Music and 18 Other Stories
After: Taras and Theron, Beyond Jerusalem

The Dead Man Series
(With Lee Goldberg and William Rabkin)
The Dead Woman

CALLSIGN:
BISHOP

PROLOGUE

Somewhere in the Kavir Desert, Semnan Province, Iran

Aziz and Muhaddar walked across the superheated ground and through the occasional scraggly brush. Above them, the sun blazed down from the hot Iranian sky, baking the earth and the dying vegetation and making the trek nearly impossible to bear, but neither man wanted to go back. Jihadists had taken over their village and accused nearly all the men of collaborating with the West. Shouts of "infidel" had split the air along with the sound of gunshots and the screams of the dying. Aziz and Muhaddar, not wanting anything to do with the Jihad, had simply run. A few bullets came close, but none touched them, and before long, they were far from their doomed village.

Of course, trekking through the sun-baked lands in central Iran wasn't an ideal escape. As the heat rose from the ground in visible waves, Aziz began to wonder whether maybe they should have stayed. At least the jihadists would have killed them quickly. Better that than a slow, painful death in the desert. Already his body felt heavy, even though he knew he'd lost weight. After only one day, he had trouble putting one leg in front of the other. His arms and legs felt sluggish and weak, and there was no water or food in sight. Maybe Muhaddar was right. Maybe they should travel at night. It would be cold, but maybe that would be for the best.

Not that it would make much difference. Without water, they had no chance.

Aziz was just starting to consider turning around to face the jihadists when Muhaddar spoke.

"Look," Muhaddar said. "Over there. A building."

"It is not real," Aziz said, not even raising his eyes. He'd seen enough mirages already.

"No, look," Muhaddar said, grabbing Aziz by the chin and forcing his face up. "I tell you, there is a building there. See?"

Aziz squinted, looking in the direction his friend pointed. At first, he could see nothing but the waves of heat radiating up from the ground, but after a minute, he spotted something. It looked like a large, squat box half buried in the earth. The sun reflected off a shiny panel on top of the box. A solar panel, maybe? Maybe it *was* a building. What better place to use a solar panel than the middle of the desert?

"Perhaps they have water," Muhaddar said.

The thought of water made Aziz's mouth ache. His throat felt so dry he thought it would crack open at any moment. "Perhaps, but who are they? And what are they doing here?"

"Does it matter?"

Aziz thought about his village. The images of the slaughter came to his mind. Bodies falling into the street, hands clutching their wounds as they cried out in pain and fear. Blood splattering the buildings as more and more people died, many of them women and children. Only a few moments ago, he'd been considering walking back to his village to face the same fate.

"No," he replied. "It does not matter."

Together they trudged through the sand, making their way to the squat building. As they grew closer, Aziz realized his initial impression that the building was half buried was not far from the truth. The part they could see was a squat round cylinder made of concrete. The rest was hidden below the surface, leaving only the cylinder visible.

As they approached, he expected to hear shouts, or shots, but none came. Soon they stood directly in front of the structure. There was no door, but a set of steel bars embedded in the concrete formed the rungs of a ladder that went to the top. After exchanging a glance with Muhaddar, Aziz grabbed the first rung and pulled himself upward, climbing toward the top.

A steel door sat on the roof like the hatch of a submarine. The shiny surface he'd seen from a distance turned out to be a small solar panel, after all. Words were stamped into the metal door, but they were written in a language neither man could read.

"Is that American writing?" Muhaddar asked.

"I don't know," Aziz replied. "It could be."

Aziz had never learned to speak or read English, but some of the characters did resemble the writing he'd seen on television the few times he'd watched American programs. That didn't necessarily mean the building was American, however. It just meant the builders used the same letters as the Americans. Just above the steel door was a symbol he thought he had seen before. It looked like three crescent moons arranged in a triangle with their backs touching. A solid circle ran through all three moons, with an empty space in the exact center of the image:

He didn't know what it meant, but the symbol filled him with a sense of foreboding.

"Maybe we should not bother them," he said.

"Water," Muhaddar replied. "What if they have water?"

Aziz looked back the way they had come. The desert stretched away in every direction; it was a flat, barren stretch of land dotted here and there by an occasional bush struggling to stay alive. Without help, they would not last another day.

Maybe the symbol meant nothing.

"Very well," he said. "Open the door."

Muhaddar pulled on the hatch, but it didn't move. After a moment, he grunted, and Aziz could see the strain in his muscles. The door lifted up about an inch. Muhaddar was normally the stronger of the two, but a day spent wandering the desert with neither food nor water had made them both weak. Aziz stepped over to help, and together they lifted the steel plate up enough to reveal a metal ladder leading down into darkness.

"Hello?" Aziz yelled into the opening. "Is there anyone here? We need water."

No answer.

Aziz looked at his friend, who nodded.

"Go," Muhaddar said. "Whatever is down there is sure to be better than what is up here."

Aziz agreed. He grabbed the rung of the ladder and started down. Muhaddar followed just after him.

The ladder descended about twenty-five feet below the door, and the lower they went, the cooler the air became. Aziz couldn't contain a relieved sigh as his feet touched the floor of the building. He marveled at how wonderful the cool air felt on his skin. "I could stay here for a week," he said.

"I may never leave," Muhaddar replied.

Aziz looked around. They stood in the center of a large chamber filled with machines and computers. To his right stood a bank of monitors showing what he assumed to be other areas of the structure as well as a few that showed the area outside the entrance. Banks of electronics blinked and beeped all around him, and on the far wall, a set of steel doors led deeper into the building. Just to his left was a large map of the facility. It showed the entrance, as well as the room they were standing in, and more. The facility was much larger than he thought it would be, and he wondered who had built it here and how they did it. The map might have held a clue, but all the words were written in American. Everything was labeled, but he could not read any of it.

Then something on the map caught his eye. A small blue square with a picture of a fork and a spoon in the middle. He knew what that meant: food. And if there was food there, there would probably be water, as well.

"Aziz," Muhaddar said, "Is that what I think it is?"

Aziz nodded. "It looks like a cafeteria or a break room."

"I wonder if there is any food there," Muhaddar said.

"Let's find out."

They walked further into the facility, waiting for someone to stop them and demand to know what they were doing there, but no one did. Here and there, Aziz spotted a few dark brown stains on the walls and floor, but he couldn't identify them. He was just beginning to wonder what had happened to the people who built this place when Muhaddar stopped and pointed at a glass window.

"Look!" Muhaddar said.

Aziz looked through the glass into a small, square room lined with shelves and documents. Glass jars of every shape and size cluttered the shelves, although many were empty or broken. Some of the documents had been ripped from the wall, and more of the brown stains spotted the room. One of them, in the shape of a hand, sent a chill up his spine. He realized then what the brown stains were: blood. He wondered again what had happened to the people who built the place.

But Muhaddar did not seem to notice any of it. His attention was fixed on a large white refrigerator in the middle of the far wall.

"Do you think there is something to drink in there?" he asked.

Without waiting for an answer, Muhaddar pulled open the door to the room and ran to the refrigerator. On the front of the refrigerator door was painted the same triple moon symbol Aziz had seen on the outside of the building. What did it mean? He wished he could remember.

"Wait," Aziz said. "I do not think it is safe."

"Praise Allah!" Muhaddar shouted, ignoring him.

Inside the refrigerator were rows and rows of plastic bottles, each of them filled with clear, cold water. Muhaddar grabbed two and threw one to Aziz, and then he opened his and started gulping down the water so fast Aziz could hear him swallowing from ten feet away.

Aziz examined the bottle in his hands. The label was white, with black writing, but in the center was that same symbol.

He looked at it closely, not knowing what it meant but sure it was not good, especially given the many bloodstains all over the facility. But the bottle in his hand was so cold. Condensation had already started to form on the outside, and moisture dripped over his fingers. His dry, raw throat begged him to take a drink. He unscrewed the cap and brought the bottle to his lips.

Muhaddar's scream startled him, and he almost dropped the bottle.

"Who are you?" Muhaddar asked, his voice tight and his eyes wide. He was staring right at Aziz as though they had not known each other their whole lives. "What are you doing here? Where is Aziz?"

"Muhaddar? Are you well?"

"Where is Aziz?" Muhaddar shouted, his face twisting in anger. A line of drool dangled from his lower lip, but he didn't seem to notice. His face looked flush, his eyes bloodshot, and his whole body trembled. "What have you done with Aziz?"

"What are you talking about?"

Muhaddar launched himself forward, grabbing Aziz by the throat and knocking him to the ground. The bottle of water flew from Aziz's hand as he and his friend toppled over onto the concrete, spilling its contents across the floor as it rolled away.

Aziz's head banged on the floor, causing his vision to go white with pain. When it returned to normal, he found himself staring up at his lifelong friend and fighting for breath under Muhaddar's crushing grip.

"Muhaddar," he gasped. "What are you doing?"

"Where…is…Aziz?" Muhaddar shouted, banging Aziz's head on the floor with every syllable. "What did you do with him?"

"Muhaddar," Aziz croaked. "I *am* Aziz. Don't you know me?"

"Lies!" Muhaddar pistoned his arms back and forward, bashing Aziz's head on the floor again and again, choking the breath from his friend's body.

Aziz tried again to reason with Muhaddar, but he couldn't find the breath to speak. He was starting to feel woozy and tired.

The last thing he saw was the crazed, furious face of his lifelong friend as his head hit the floor one last time, then everything went dark.

1.

Pinckney, NH.

The small, single engine Cessna rolled to a slow, rough stop. The potholes in the asphalt caused the cabin to bounce and jerk, spilling the passenger's drink in his lap. Cold coffee, several hours old and barely touched. On either side of the pocked runway, a short grass field extended for fifty or so yards before giving way to a huge green forest of maples, birches and assorted evergreens. The scent of pine filtered in through the plane's vents, mixing with the smells of coffee and aftershave.

"Son of a bitch," the passenger said, trying to dry his pants with a napkin with little success. "Good thing it wasn't hot."

"Small favors," said the pilot.

"Yeah, yeah. Thank God for 'em."

The pilot chuckled. "As well you should, Mr. Duncan."

"Don't start, Billings."

Billings turned his face away, but not before Duncan saw the smirk on his face. *Sanctimonious SOB*, he thought.

"Looks like your ride is here," Billings said, pointing out the starboard window.

Tom Duncan, former President of the United States, shifted in his seat to look right. The Cessna didn't have much for windows—or passenger space, for that matter—but he was able to spot a single black SUV rolling its way up a thin gravel road toward the plane. Other than Billings, only one other person on the planet knew Duncan was coming to Pinckney.

Jacobs, Duncan thought. *Let's see what's so important.*

Eli Jacobs headed Duncan's cleanup team at the site of the old Manifold Genetics lab nearby. Jacobs and his men were responsible for going through Manifold's records, storage facilities, computers and anything else they found to try to figure out just what the hell Ridley had been doing. With all the strange genetic experiments Manifold was involved in, it was often difficult to keep track of everything. Judging by the spotty record keeping in the Manifold *Alpha* lab, even the Manifold employees had had trouble sorting through all the data.

But Jacobs had found something. He wouldn't have called Duncan if it wasn't important. Not long ago, Duncan would have had to fly to the site in a large private helicopter. Two fighter jets would have flown escort and it would have been impossible to hide his presence from the locals. Those days were long gone. He had even waived his right to a Secret Service detail. Now he was as anonymous as it gets, sitting on an overgrown, pothole-filled runway in the backwater of New Hampshire. The tiny Cessna would have fit easily inside the belly of Air Force One.

Duncan smiled a bittersweet smile, then moved toward the door.

It's better this way, he told himself. *The chains are broken.* He was free now to pursue his role as Deep Blue, Chess Team's handler, mentor and operations eye-in-the-sky, without the constraints of his former role as President getting in the way.

He stepped out of the plane and into the field just as the

passenger door on the SUV opened. Eli Jacobs, a balding, pudgy man with black horn rim glasses, stepped out of the truck and waved. Jacobs wore his usual white coat over black pants. His breast pocket bulged with a wide assortment of pens, at least six of them. As he waddled over, Duncan was struck by the idea that Jacobs was the poster boy for the American nerd. Short, socially inept and brilliant.

"Mr. President," Jacobs said, saluting. "I—"

"Please," Duncan interrupted, "I'm not the President anymore. And stop saluting me, Eli."

Eli's hand dropped. "Perhaps, but people still call Bill Clinton 'Mr. President,' and he's been out of office for years."

"Different circumstances."

"All right, Mr. Duncan. I need to show you something back at the lab."

"I'm fine, Eli. How are you?" Duncan asked, trying not to smile.

Eli missed the subtle attempt at humor. "I'm not well, Mr. President. Not well at all. And you won't be either. Not after I show you what we found."

△ △ △

Duncan followed Jacobs into a sterile lab deep underground. Like most of Manifold's bases, the *Alpha* facility lay almost completely buried inside a mountain, making it invisible to satellite photos using the visible spectrum. Fortunately, modern satellites were equipped with a wide array of cameras, including infrared, radar, x-ray, gamma, and a few others that only Duncan and a handful of others knew existed. These technologies made it possible to map at least the top levels of the facility from the safety of the Thermosphere.

Prior to leaving for Pinckney, Duncan spent some time

going over the maps of Manifold *Alpha* produced by ground-penetrating radar. The illustrations revealed the facility was hundreds of feet deep—and that was not counting the natural cavern underneath it. But Duncan had a feeling they had yet to truly uncover the scope of the expansive base. How it was built on U.S. soil without being noticed was beyond him, but he suspected a good number of New Hampshire officials made large deposits to their bank accounts. While those officials would normally be investigated and prosecuted, this time secrecy demanded they be left alone. None of that bothered Duncan as much as the facility's still-unexplored depths.

What was Ridley doing down here? As Jacobs motioned him over to a large, flat screen computer monitor, he realized he was about to find out.

"Look at this," Jacobs said.

Duncan stepped around and looked at the computer screen. It showed a picture of a wheat stalk. Near the top of the stalk was a pair of dark, roughly triangular masses, which looked almost like a fungus. "What am I looking at?" Duncan asked.

"The sclerotial stage of *Claviceps Purpurea*, otherwise known as ergot."

"Sclerotial? What does that mean?"

"Not important. You should be focusing on the ergot."

"I thought that was part of a horse's hoof," Duncan said, confused.

"Different ergot. This one is a fungus. A dangerous one."

"Explain."

Jacobs punched a button on the keypad and the screen shifted to an illustration. To Duncan it looked like a random grouping of hexagons and tiny circles.

It took him a moment to realize he was looking at a large and complex molecule.

"What is that?" Duncan asked.

"That is the molecule of *ergotamine*, a complex alkaloid found in ergot, and just one of the many such alkaloids contained in the fungus. The effects of ergotamine on the human system are wide and varied, but include vivid hallucinations, irrational behavior, convulsions and even death. Mankind has been using it as a poison for thousands of years. The ancient Assyrians used it to poison the wells of their enemies as far back as 2400 BC."

"What was Ridley doing with it?"

Jacobs pulled up another screen. This one showed a molecule similar to the first, with one difference.

"What is M-Erg 2.6.3?" Duncan asked.

"An additive," Jacobs replied. "Manifold altered the molecule."

"What does it do?"

"We don't know," Jacobs said. "The lab is still analyzing it, but we're having trouble separating it from the rest of the molecule."

Duncan knew enough about molecules to know that even a tiny alteration could drastically change the characteristics of anything. Once you started fooling around with substances on a molecular level, anything was possible. Based on Manifold's history, Duncan was pretty sure that whatever M-Erg 2.6.3 was, it didn't help crops grow or fight off cancer cells. More likely, Ridley had intended to use it to further his own agenda.

"How about an educated guess?" Duncan asked.

"Well, obviously M-Erg stands for Manifold Ergotamine. The numbers probably refer to the version used, like in software. That means they've been working on this for a while, so its intended use was clearly defined somewhere in the database."

"Okay."

"Given Ridley's other works, he was probably trying to enhance the ergotamine. Most likely trying to make it more potent or volatile. Ergot has some medicinal uses, some of which carry over into Ridley's genetic attempts at immortality. It might have something to do with his manipulations of the Hydra's blood. Some of my staff theorize that he used the alkaloids to stop or stall the Hydra's regenerative processes at different stages, which would help him to observe the changes and document them."

Jacobs almost sounded like he was trying to convince himself of his own words.

"But you don't agree, do you?" Duncan asked.

Jacobs turned his chair around. "No. I don't."

"Why not?"

"Well, it's just that ergot is a potent substance already, and ergotamine is nasty stuff. Not only that, but there are plenty of other poisons, including several powerful neurotoxins, that can instantly halt biological activity, many of which are readily available to labs and don't require any alteration. If you ask me, I think he meant to use this on people. Probably after building that 'New World' of his."

Duncan shook his head. The revelation should have been shocking, but when Richard Ridley and Manifold Genetics were involved, shocking was standard operating procedure. "What would that do to people?"

"I don't know. In its regular form, ergotamine is similar to LSD. Enhanced? Who knows? Maybe instant death or severe brain damage. Without the rest of the data, the only way to find out would be to test it on someone."

"Let's not."

"Agreed."

"So is this why you called me here? You could have told me this over the phone, Eli."

"Not exactly. The weaponized ergotamine is bad, but it's not the worst part."

"It gets worse?"

"I'm afraid so." Jacobs pulled a manila folder off the table and handed it to Duncan. "Read this."

Duncan opened the file and started to read. Less than two paragraphs in, he felt the blood drain from his face. By the time he finished the first page and looked at the pictures, he had seen enough. He closed the folder and handed it back.

"How recent is this? Are you sure it's not old data?"

"It's dated two days before the raid on this facility. Ridley probably never had a chance to act on it since he was fighting off Sigler's team at the time."

"I have to go," Duncan turned and walked briskly out of the lab, not wanting to waste any time. He needed to get to a secure line as soon as possible, and he didn't trust any of the phones in Manifold *Alpha*. Some of them could be tainted still, or monitored. The entire facility was in the process of being retrofitted for Chess Team's use, but until the job was complete, he couldn't take that chance. Too many lives were at stake.

2.

Erik Somers—Callsign: Bishop, sat in front of his computer, waiting for a file from a contact. In his hand was a cup of green tea sweetened with stevia. The contact, who Bishop knew as CJ—an undercover operative who had supplied valuable intel in the past—had e-mailed him the day before, claiming to have some news for him. Bishop knew CJ was currently in Iran investigating suspected terrorist cells, but he couldn't figure out what it might have to do with him. Contacting him directly was a breach of protocol, especially now that Bishop was no longer officially part of Delta. For all intents and purposes, Chess Team no longer existed. The team hadn't just been disbanded, they had ceased to exist. Records of the team's actions were deleted, and the team members' military records ended just before they joined Chess Team, listing each as KIA. *Killed in action.* There were plenty of people who had personal experience with the team, like CJ, who knew, or could guess better, but any official inquiry into the team would come up blank.

It was all smoke and mirrors. Chess Team still existed, only now they were off the government radar. They had gone from an elite Delta team to strictly Black Ops, which gave them a heck of a lot more freedom to do their jobs. Not having the government sniffing around their every move freed them up to be more creative in dealing with threats to the country. Of course, the same lack of support also made the job more dangerous, because whenever they went out they had only themselves to rely on. Still, Bishop preferred it that way. At least now, they could act without the risk of public exposure.

The computer beeped, and Bishop looked up. The message he'd been waiting for popped up on the screen:

INCOMING FILE FROM CALLSIGN JOKER.
ACCEPT? Y/N

"Joker" was CJ's official callsign. It probably had something to do with his group name, but Bishop didn't know. He'd never even met the man face to face. Sometimes Black Ops were like that. He typed Y on the keyboard.

The fiber-optic connection downloaded the 2 MB file in less than a second, and it opened on a picture of a Middle Eastern couple sitting at the table. They looked to be in their late fifties or early sixties, and appeared to be sitting down to dinner. The woman's face was clearly visible, indicating the pair were either moderate Muslims or in their own home. Judging by the setting—which seemed to be a large, private dining area—Bishop assumed the latter.

But what could these two middle aged Muslims have to do with him?

He read the caption attached to the photo.

DAWOUD AND FAIZA ABBASI, 23052011 18:27 IRST.
SvPh #1138-7A

He checked the tag at the back of the caption. 23052011 was a date: April 23, 2011, and IRST stood for Iran Standard

Time. SvPh stood for Surveillance Photo. That meant whoever had snapped the picture had taken it in secret at 6:27 pm in Iran over four months ago. Judging by the number attached, it was one of many such photos of the couple.

But who were they?

Bishop typed a message into the computer. *What does this have to do with me?* Then he hit SEND.

While he waited, he examined the couple again. They looked like any ordinary Muslim couple sitting down to eat. The man was large and broad, with a curved, hawk-like nose that gave his face an overall predatory appearance. The hair at his temples had gone to gray, but the rest of it remained jet black. His eyes were a deep brown, wrinkled at the corners in what might have been a smile if not for the stern, disapproving curve of his lips.

The woman sat to his right. Her skin was dark and her face narrow, and like her husband, her dark black hair was turning to gray. But where his face was hard and angular, hers was soft and kind, and perhaps a little sad. Her brown eyes were on the table in front of them rather than on her husband, and she held her hands folded demurely in her lap, waiting for her husband to eat first. The two were the only people in the picture. If Dawoud Abbasi had any other wives, they were not present.

Bishop sipped at his tea, willing the image to make sense. Something about the woman looked familiar, but he couldn't put his finger on it. He zoomed the picture in, centering the image on her face. Did he know her? If so, from where? He felt like he could almost place her features, but each time he tried he just missed the connection.

When the computer beeped again, a new window popped up on the screen. Since he had already accepted a transmission from Joker, the computer assumed the sender was safe and didn't ask for acceptance a second time, thus the message appeared right in front of his face.

THEY ARE YOUR PARENTS.

The mug of tea shattered on the floor.

△ △ △

The phone rang three times before a gruff, scratchy voice answered. "Keasling speaking. What can I do for you, Mr. President?"

"Stop calling me that," Duncan said.

"No can do, sir. Now what's the problem?"

"Is your line secure?"

"Of course."

"It's Manifold."

"Again? Damn Ridley. He's a real pain in the ass. Where is he now?"

"It's not him this time," Duncan said. "Manifold was working on what we believe to be a weaponized form of ergot poisoning. They never finished it because the team infiltrated the facility before they could."

"*Weaponized* ergot?" Keasling asked. "You mean, Ridley made the stuff *more* dangerous?"

"What do you know about ergot?"

"It's a nasty poison. Been around for thousands of years. Used in warfare as far back as 2400 BC. The Assyrians used to—"

"Right. That's the stuff," Duncan said. He should have known Keasling would know all about ergot's military history. "Manifold was working on an additive."

"But you said Chess Team shut them down. That sounds like good news to me. What's the problem?"

"The problem is Manifold put one of their research labs in the middle of the Kavir Desert."

"Iran? Why would Ridley build there?"

"Best guess? To be close to their potential clientele. Plus, if something went wrong it would be written off as an Iranian weapons lab."

"Makes sense."

"But something went wrong," Duncan continued. "Two weeks before the raid on the *Alpha* facility, a climate-controlled storage bunker in Iran was raided by jihadists, who discovered it while chasing down a pair of local men. It didn't take long for them to realize what they had found. I have some video footage from the bunker's security camera showing a group of them carrying out gallons on the stuff."

"Are you telling me that a group of Islamic radicals in Iran has a cache of weaponized ergot?"

"That's exactly what I am telling you."

"Damn," Keasling said.

"How is Bishop?" Duncan asked. While the team was no longer officially Delta, they still lived at Fort Bragg and would move to their new quarters at the *Alpha* facility later in the year. While Duncan oversaw the progress at *Alpha*, Keasling kept an eye on the team and sometimes reprised his middleman role. But Duncan was still on top of things and knew Bishop was the only team member not currently deployed or on personal leave. "Think he's up to it?"

"You know Bishop," Keasling said. "No matter how beat up the guy gets, he's impossible to read."

Bishop had fallen victim to one of Ridley's experiments that left him with incredible regenerative capabilities but had nearly driven him mad. A crystal with strange healing properties recovered from Mount Meru in Vietnam had helped control the rage, but he'd endured physical injuries—a removed arm, near decapitation, repeated drowning—that took a toll on the human psyche, even one as tough as Bishop's. The team's last mission had stripped Bishop of his regenerative abilities, and the madness that came with them, but the memories of his injuries, and the madness, had to be haunting him.

"Think he's ready for a trip to Iran?" Duncan asked.

"As luck would have it, he came to see me this morning, asking for exactly that."

3.

The cabin of the Boeing 737 was much too quiet for his taste. Bishop was used to traveling in the Crescent, which was loud even inside the cabin. But for this job he'd had to take a commercial flight to Tehran, and the two planes couldn't have been more different.

For one thing, he thought, *there aren't any computers on the walls.*

When Duncan called him and told him he would be going to Iran to look for a terrorist cell that had stolen Manifold material, he almost couldn't believe it. It seemed like too much of a coincidence, given the timing of his recent discovery. Of course, he would be landing in Tehran, in northern Iran, while Dawoud and Faiza Abbasi lived in Shiraz, some distance to the south in the Fars province. Still, at least he was in the country. If time permitted, he would make the trip south and pay them a visit.

Dawoud and Faiza Abbasi. His parents. Could it be true? Bishop knew he was adopted as a baby, but he'd never even bothered looking for his birth parents. They gave him up, and he was fine with it. As far as he was concerned, he didn't need to know them. But now that he did know, he couldn't help but feel excited at the possibility of meeting them, as well as a bit anxious.

What would they be like? Would they be happy to see him? A thousand questions ran through his mind, and he meant to ask them all, especially the most important one.

Why? Why had they given him up? The old anger threatened to bubble to the surface. Childhood memories began to play through his mind. Years of wondering what was so wrong with him that his own parents didn't want him. Didn't he measure up? Was he weak as a baby? Small? Were his eyes the wrong color? As a baby, it couldn't have been anything he'd done, so what was it? Maybe his parents just weren't ready for children. Maybe they had better things to do than raise their own blood. Maybe—

He realized he was squeezing the armrest so hard his knuckles had turned white, and he forced himself to relax. He took a slow, deep breath and reeled in his racing thoughts, slowing them to a crawl. He pictured a placid lake in the mountains. Cool, clear water. The sound of birds in the background. A laughing family in a canoe paddling their way across the surface. It was a technique he'd employed often in his attempts to manage his anger. Soon his pulse and breathing returned to normal, and he released his grip on the armrest.

I'm okay, he thought. *Still waters.*

Why had his parents given him up? The answer would have to wait. As anxious as he was to meet the Abbasis, Deep Blue had sent him to do a job. He shook his head and tried to clear his parents—his parents!—from his mind and focus on the task at hand.

Manifold had been making a stronger, more potent form of some poison called ergot. Bishop knew that ergot had been used as an effective weapon in the ancient world, but the new strain could be much, much worse. No one knew what it did, but the fact that Manifold was involved boded ill for everyone. Ridley never did things on a small scale.

But even worse than making a dangerous new bio-weapon, Manifold had let it fall into the hands of Iranian terrorists. Bishop shook his head, wondering who in the hell had let that happen. Ridley was a lot of things, but unorganized wasn't one of them. Of course, Ridley was out of the picture and without his oversight, someone in his company screwed up, or just jumped ship, and now Bishop had to clean up the mess.

Just like always.

A soft beep sounded through the cabin and a pleasant female voice came over the intercom. "Ladies and gentlemen, we are beginning our descent into Tehran. We will be landing at Imam Khomeini International Airport in five minutes. Please fasten your seat belts and ensure that all electronic devices have been turned off." The announcement repeated itself in Persian, Spanish and French.

Bishop checked his lap belt, making sure it was cinched tight, and relaxed. He'd be on the ground soon enough, and afterward he'd have to find transportation out into the Kavir Desert. He had the coordinates of the Manifold station, but getting there would be a problem. First, he'd have to get a charter flight to a small village on the edge of the Kavir, then hire a car to actually go into the desert itself. It would probably cost a pretty penny, but he was sure he could accomplish both.

Money talks, he thought. *Even in Iran, money talks.*

After his mission briefing, he'd been given over 10 million Iranian rials. Even though it only equaled about $1,000 in US currency, it should be more than enough to purchase anything he needed while in Iran, especially after he left Tehran. Should the need arise, he had access to more funds, but more likely he would simply acquire anything else he might need. His Delta training had included numerous techniques for gathering supplies, foraging, stealth and even hotwiring foreign and domestic cars. Iran was the twelfth largest manufacturer of automobiles in the world, even though few of the vehicles made in the country found their way to the US. Bishop was confident he could find a car that would get him to the Kavir Desert, even if he had to steal it.

He began to go through his checklist. First, he would need to get to the Manifold outpost and look for signs of occupation. If the site was occupied, he would try to infiltrate or identify the group. If the place was empty, he would need to go inside and see if the terrorist had left behind any clues. Most of the time, people couldn't help but leave clues behind, especially jihadists, who wanted the world to know what they had done. Bishop's next steps would be based on what he found at the site.

The plane touched down on the runway, and Bishop looked out the window. The sprawling metropolis of Tehran sat in the sun, waiting for him. Skyscrapers reached for the clouds with concrete fingers, reflecting the hot Iranian sun back from a million windows. He was too far away to hear the bustle of the city's people as they went about their day, but he could imagine it well enough. Bicycles and mopeds threading their way through cars and pedestrians. The sound of thousands of horns and millions of voices rumbling through the city streets like a wall of sound. The thick haze of smog that hovered over the city.

First time visitors to Tehran were often surprised by its modern look and vast scale. Western tourists often pictured huge, spired mosques and horse driven carts in cobbled streets filled with men in turbans and women in long black *habibs*. Bishop had been here several times and knew what to expect. Tehran was a city on the hub of the world, more populous even than London or New York, and played home to a large and diverse gathering of people. It would be easy enough for him to blend in. He was born here, after all.

The plane taxied to a stop outside its assigned gate, and after a few minutes, Bishop and the other passengers began to disembark. He shuffled down the central aisle, a prop carry-on briefcase in hand, and tried not to think about Dawoud and Faiza Abbasi.

First things first, he reminded himself. *Tend to business, then you can go to Shiraz and see what you need to see.*

Easier said than done.

△ △ △

Inside the airport, two men stood by a souvenir shop and watched as the latest round of passengers exited the gate. A steady stream of people walked through the door, including several Americans, an Asian couple, and a group of Hispanics, all walking side by side with the Muslims who belonged here and those that did not. Ordinarily the two would be watching for freedom fighters, but today was different. Today their attention was focused on one visitor in particular: a large, burly man in a dark gray suit. He looked Iranian, as well he should, but he wasn't. Not really. He was an American with an Iranian face. The two men spotted him right away.

"Is that him?" one of the men asked.

The other nodded. "It is."

"Should we go now?"

"Not yet. It is too crowded here. Wait until he is outside."

"I will call ahead and let them know we will be bringing him shortly."

The man walked through the door and into the airport. He carried a black briefcase in his right hand and a map of the airport in the other. After consulting the map, he turned to his right and started to make his way to the exit.

The two men fell into step behind the foreigner and followed him to the exit.

4.

Bishop stopped at the exit to the airport, watching as dozens of taxis vied for position outside the doors. Amidst the taxis, a large number of shuttles sat idling in the parking lot, waiting to carry passengers to one hotel or another. Private vehicles were prohibited from this area, and with good reason. With all the people milling around the waiting cabs and shuttles, there was barely enough room to breathe. He kept his eyes forward, scanning the vehicles for an empty taxi, but occasionally he glanced into nearby windows and mirrors, checking to see if the two men from the gate were still tailing him.

He'd picked up on their attention the moment he stepped off the plane. They tried to be subtle, but his years of experience, combined with his extensive training and natural paranoia, made them easy to spot. Two men of medium height and build, both dressed as laborers, had followed him to the exit. One of them had already made a call with his cell phone, so Bishop knew they had friends waiting somewhere up ahead. But what did they want with him?

There were several Americans on board the plane, most far less intimidating than Bishop. If these two men and their allies were jihadists, why didn't they latch onto one of them? Were they after him specifically? If so, did they know who he was? How? He'd chosen a commercial airliner because he wanted to get into Iran undetected and the *Crescent* was already in use. As far as he knew, only Deep Blue and Keasling knew he would be coming to Iran, so how did these guys find out?

Whoever they were, they would probably wait until after he left the airport before they tried anything. Airport security at Imam Khomeini was pretty tight, and the men would have had a hard time smuggling guns into the building. Additionally, the whole airport could be locked down in seconds if anything remotely resembling a terrorist plot were detected. So as long as he stayed in the airport, he would probably be safe. But then he would never find out who they were, not to mention that he couldn't investigate the Manifold site from an airport restroom. If he wanted to get on with his job, he would have to get going and trust his training to deal with any obstacles that might come up along the way.

Bishop spotted an empty taxi idling down the lot. The driver must have just arrived, because he was far back in the crowd of cars and shuttles and he didn't have a fare yet. Bishop tightened his grip on his briefcase and started toward the taxi. Along the way, he glanced into the windshield of a waiting shuttle. There were the two men, milling around near the exit and watching his back. He chuckled. They weren't very good at this. They might be able to stalk an unwitting tourist, but if they hoped to surprise *him*, they were going to be sorely disappointed.

Out of habit, Bishop checked the back seat of the taxi to make sure it was empty, then he swung open the door and climbed inside, watching as the two men following him climbed into another taxi about fifty yards away. His driver—a dark-skinned man with short, curly black hair and a black baseball cap—sat in the front seat, separated from the passenger compartment by a solid piece of Plexiglas, most likely bullet proof. Such things were common in Tehran, he recalled. Hell, they were common in New York and Los Angeles, too. Big cities tended to attract crime, no matter where in the world they were located.

"The Evin Hotel," Bishop said in Persian, referring to a newly renovated hotel about half an hour from the airport. Once there he would change into different clothes and hire transportation out to the Kavir. He thought about how the two men had been waiting for him and realized he couldn't come back to Imam Khomeini for a while. He'd have to look for charter planes leaving one of Tehran's other airports.

The driver nodded and put the car into gear. A minute later, they were speeding and bobbing through airport traffic as the driver weaved and honked his way out of the Imam Khomeini complex. Bishop lost sight of the men following him, but he reasoned that they probably lost sight of him, as well. Good.

Of course, if they *did* know who he was and why he was here, then it wouldn't matter. Somewhere up ahead, their friends would be waiting for him. He would just have to be ready.

Outside the airport grounds, the traffic didn't improve. The driver switched lanes at random and cut back and forth between other cars trying to make headway, but it was still slow going. Tehran was home to over 8 million people, and such a large number made travel through the city itself inherently slow going, especially at certain times of the day.

After about an hour, Bishop spotted the street leading to the Evin Hotel. He'd been there before a few years earlier, and he'd been to Tehran enough times to have a good working knowledge of the city's layout, so he was a bit surprised when the driver passed right by the street.

"You should have turned left at that last light," he offered, again speaking Persian.

"I don't think so," the driver said in English. "We lost your tail back at the airport, but they'll look for you at a place like the Evin. It's too obvious. I'm taking you somewhere else."

For a moment, Bishop was too stunned to speak, then everything clicked into place. In addition to Keasling and Deep Blue, there was one other person who knew Bishop would be coming to Iran. But he would have expected that person to be in Shiraz.

"Nice to meet you, Joker," Bishop said.

"Call me CJ," the driver replied, smiling.

"How did you know I would be coming to Tehran?"

CJ chuckled, and Bishop took the hint. CJ knew, and that's all there was to it. He would never reveal the source of his intel, any more than Bishop would. He smiled.

"All right, then. Where are we going?" Bishop asked.

"There is a plane waiting to fly us both out to a small village on the outskirts of the Kavir. You have the coordinates of the Manifold facility, right?"

Bishop nodded.

"Good," CJ continued. "The village is called Hassi. There's not much left of it, but I know a guy there who can arrange transportation for us into the desert."

"Not much left of it? Why? What happened?"

"The men who found the Manifold site also stormed through the village. They didn't leave much behind."

"But there's a guy with a car?"

"A ride," CJ corrected. "I never said anything about a car. How are your riding skills, anyway?"

Bishop shrugged. "I can get by."

CJ smiled. "I bet."

"Those guys were waiting for me, weren't they?" Bishop asked. "They know who I am and why I'm here."

CJ nodded. "And they have friends. Lots of them. And all of them want to talk to you."

"What do they want with me?"

"You remember that picture I sent you of Dawoud and Faiza Abbasi?"

Bishop nodded. Of course, he remembered.

"Did you ever ask yourself why the United States Government would have such a picture? Why would a Delta team place cameras inside the home of an Iranian citizen and then monitor his activities?"

Bishop hadn't considered that. He had assumed the picture was a fluke occurrence. But now that he thought about it, it didn't make sense. The picture had been taken from inside the Abbasi home. Why would the US Government be spying on the Abbasis in their house? Unless…

"Damn," he said.

"Yup," CJ replied. "I hate to be the one to break it to you, Bishop, but your biological father is a terrorist."

△ △ △

Several miles from the airport, another taxi slowed to a stop outside the Evin Hotel. Two men stepped out of the backseat. One of them went around to the front to pay the driver, while the other pulled out a cell phone and made a call.

"Yes, he is here," he said into the phone. "No, we do not have him. He hired a taxi at Imam Khomeini before we could…of course we followed him, but our driver was not… At this moment? We are at the Evin Hotel. Ahmad believes the man might be staying here. Do not worry. If he is here, we will find him and bring him to you."

Ahmad stepped toward the rear of the taxi as the car sped away, putting his wallet back into his pocket. He started to speak, but closed his mouth once his partner pointed to the phone.

"I will," the man said. "I will. I assure you, we will find him. Do not worry."

The first man closed his phone and looked at Ahmad. "He is not happy."

"I did not think he would be," Ahmad said. "What did he say, Massai?"

Massai shoved the phone into his pocket. "He said we better find Somers soon, or it will be very bad for us." He narrowed his eyes and stared at Ahmad, wanting to make sure his partner understood his full meaning. "*Very* bad."

Ahmad paled, then nodded his head. "Understood. We should get to work, then."

The two men turned toward the entrance of the Evin Hotel and started walking.

"Do you think he is here?" Ahmad asked.

"I hope so," Massai replied. "For our sake."

"And if he is not?"

Massai shook his head. "We will keep looking. We dare not return without him."

5.

Bishop felt like CJ had just punched him in the gut. "You sure?"

"Oh, yeah," CJ said, weaving around a slow moving truck. "No question. We've been watching him for a long time. He's not just a terrorist, he's also a top terrorist recruiter. He spent several years recruiting for Al Quaeda, among others. He's pretty high up the food chain."

"Why haven't you taken him in?"

"No proof."

Bishop snorted. "This isn't *Law and Order*. What's the real reason?"

CJ looked back at him via the rearview mirror and laughed. "All right, you got me. The reason we don't take him down is that we like Dawoud Abbasi right where he is. As long as he doesn't suspect that we're wise to him, we can completely monitor his operations and keep tabs on every new terrorist he recruits. We've been able to neutralize quite a few potential threats with this information. Just last year a finger of Al Quaeda was planning another series of hijackings, but because we were able to stay on top of the people involved and put a stop to it. Probably saved thousands of lives. We—"

"All right," Bishop said. "I get the picture. Abbasi is more valuable out here than behind bars."

"You better believe it."

"What about…" Bishop found the word difficult, but he spat it out anyway, "…my mother. What about her?"

"She's clean, as near as we can tell. Dawoud has nine other wives, several of which are actively involved in his recruiting processes—record keeping, contacting families, that sort of thing—but Faiza stays clear of it. She seems to dislike that side of her husband a great deal, and contrary to the accepted norms of Iranian society, she has voiced her displeasure with her husband's work many times. To be honest, we aren't sure why Dawoud keeps her around at all."

"Why he doesn't kill her, you mean," Bishop stated.

CJ nodded. "Exactly." He sped through a red light, earning a chorus of honks from irritated drivers as he passed. He stuck his hand out the driver's side window and gave them a gesture that made them honk even more, though Bishop couldn't see it from his seat. "His personal life would be a lot simpler without her in the picture."

"Other children?"

"Dawoud has plenty, but Faiza only had one."

"Me."

"Yup. You." CJ nodded, then laid on the horn and stuck his head out the window to swear at another driver in perfect Persian. The other driver said something back, and CJ called him an asshole—in English—and withdrew his head. "You're his first, too. The eldest son. The heir to his empire, so to speak."

"His empire?"

"Didn't I tell you? The Abbasis are rich. Worth over half a billion dollars."

Bishop's eyebrows rose. "That's a lot of money."

"Damn straight."

"How'd you find all this out?"

"You know I can't tell you that."

They rode on in silence for a while. Bishop watched CJ dart and honk his way through Tehran traffic until they left the city limits, then he steered the car onto Freeway 7.

"Are we going to Qom?" Bishop asked, referring to the large city about a hundred miles south of Tehran.

"No, just heading south. Our plane is waiting for us in a hangar about 20 minutes outside of Tehran."

"You've arranged it already?"

"I knew you'd be coming."

"Because of my parents?" The word felt strange on his tongue, like trying to pick up a quarter while wearing gloves. "They're in Shiraz, not Tehran."

"Because of Manifold," CJ replied. "The best place to fly in to get close to the Kavir is Tehran, unless you want to pretend you're making a holy pilgrimage to Qom. You're not a Shi'a Muslim, though."

"I'm not Muslim at all."

"Exactly, which is why I knew you'd pick Tehran. And Imam Khomeini is the biggest airport in the city for international flights, so I figured you'd come there if you were flying commercial."

"What if I'd flown military?"

"Then I'd still be waiting, wouldn't I?"

Bishop shrugged. CJ had guessed commercial and knew to check Imam Khomeini over the other airports in Tehran. That was probably how the other men had found him, too. They were probably part of the same terrorist group that had taken over the Manifold site. Most likely, they had placed agents at all four of Tehran's major airports to watch for him. That would explain why the men were there waiting. But one question bothered him more than how well they predicted his arrival: how did they know he'd be coming?

The question hung in his mind as CJ exited Freeway 7 and turned onto a small access road headed east. In the distance, Bishop saw the mountains that bordered the Kavir Desert, or Dasht-e Kavir, as it was known in Iran. In the US, people usually pictured large, ever changing sand dunes when they imagined a desert, but that wasn't always the case. People often forgot that the entire continent of Antarctica is actually classified as a desert.

Named after the many salt marshes, or *kavir*, that could be found within it, the Kavir Desert stretched from the Alborz mountain range in the northwest to the Dasht-e Lut, or Lut Desert, in the southeast and took up a land area of about 30,000 square miles. At its heart lay the Great Kavir, a salt marsh over 150 miles long.

"The Manifold site isn't in the middle of the Rig-e Jenn, is it?" Bishop asked, referring to the large area of the Kavir Desert that did consist of the sand dunes and desolation most people associated with a desert climate. Very few people ventured into the area. The old caravan travelers believed it to be a place where evil spirits waited, and even today, many of the people who lived in the nearby areas of the Kavir avoided it for the same reason.

CJ scoffed. "If it was, we'd never get there. No one has ever successfully explored the place. The closest anyone has come was when that Austrian geographer crossed the southern tail of it in the 1930's. Gabriel, I think his name was. No, the Manifold site is just over a day's walk from Hassi, a village just south of the Alborz Mountains. The land is hot and dry, but no sand dunes."

Bishop smiled. He, of course, knew all along that the Manifold site wasn't in the Rig-e Jenn. His briefing from Deep Blue had told him exactly where the site was located. He even had the exact latitude and longitude. He was just wondering how much CJ knew. Apparently, the man knew plenty. Was his team investigating the Manifold site, as well?

Since Bishop's team had gone from Delta to Black Ops, it was certainly possible. For all intents and purposes, Chess Team didn't exist anymore, so if anyone in power were to investigate Manifold, they would have to use another Special Forces team—one sanctioned by the US government. Domenick Boucher at CIA and General Keasling were supposed to redirect any intel on Manifold to Deep Blue, but there was always the possibility that another Delta team or even a division of the CIA could stumble across something, and act on it, before the higher-ups were informed. Is that what was happening here?

Maybe. But he knew he would never get that information out of CJ. He made a mental note to ask Deep Blue the next time he spoke with him.

"Here we are," CJ said, turning onto a small dirt road.

At the end of the road, Bishop saw a large metal building with wide doors. From the road, the building was hidden by a large copse of trees, but as they drew closer, it came fully into view. Bishop recognized it as a small hangar. The doors stood open to reveal a tan Cessna 172. The closer they got to the hangar, the more of the plane he could see, and the sight wasn't as encouraging as he'd first hoped.

The Cessna had clearly seen better days. The paint was faded in more places than not, and the once black stripe along the side was now gray. Several of the panels on the fuselage and wings were a different color than the rest of the plane, indicating they'd been replaced but never repainted, and here and there, he spotted the rough welds of hasty patch jobs. The windows looked dirty, and the whole plane needed a wash. The airframe seemed sound from the car, but he wouldn't know for sure until he got a closer look. Even then, Bishop was no airplane mechanic. He knew how to fly them and how to jump out of them, and that's where his knowledge ended.

"Looks old," he said.

"It is," CJ replied. "Older than you. It's one of the first models from back in 1956. Over twenty five thousand hours logged on the airframe. It's got a new engine, though, and updated electronics. It'll get us there."

"You know the pilot?" Bishop asked, still looking at the plane.

"Oh, yeah. I know him real well," CJ replied. "He's me."

Bishop grinned. He might have known.

They came to a stop beside the barn and both men stepped out of the car. Bishop stood looking at the plane, marveling at how something that looked so old and patched could still fly. It sure wasn't the Crescent.

"How long will it take to get to Hassi?" Bishop asked.

"Not long," CJ replied. "An hour. Maybe an hour and a half if the wind is against us. The plane looks like a warm turd, but it can move."

Bishop nodded. "When do we leave?"

"How about right now?"

Nothing like getting right down to business. "All right," Bishop said. "Let's move." He reached up and grabbed the door handle on the Cessna's fuselage, then pulled it open. It seemed much smaller inside than he'd anticipated. But then again, it had been a very long time since he'd flown in a single-engine prop plane. The Crescent had room for row upon row of computers and equipment, and commercial airliners were huge, if cramped. CJ's Cessna had enough room for four passengers, as long as they were built like Miley Cyrus. He worked his way around the tiny rear passenger seats until he reached the front of the plane, then he sat in the co-pilot's spot. CJ came up behind him and closed the cabin door. Then he took his place in the pilot's seat.

CJ started the plane. The engine came to life right away, and to Bishop's surprise, it was smooth and quiet. He'd been expecting backfires and heavy vibration, but the plane eased out of the hangar without a single hiccup.

CJ must have noticed the expression on his face, because he turned to Bishop and nodded toward the engine. "Told you. I installed a brand new engine last year. Less than a hundred hours on this one. And it's an upgrade over the stock setup. 210 hp instead of the normal 180, although the original engine only had 145. This thing is updated where it counts, B. It'll get us where we need to go."

"I didn't say anything," Bishop replied. "A plane's a plane."

"You were thinking it," CJ said.

CJ steered the plane onto a grass runway and gave it some gas. The plane bumped along the runway but soon lifted into the air. "What'd I tell you? Smooth as silk."

Bishop nodded. "Good." He looked through the window at the ground below, watching as it fell away. Whenever he flew in the Crescent, he was always in the back where there were no windows, so this was something new. As the ground got farther and farther away, he thought about his former regenerative abilities. A gift from Richard Ridley, he'd been able to march into just about anything without fear of being hurt. Those days were gone, now. Ridley had taken the ability away as easily as he'd given it. He would have to learn to be careful again.

"You all right, B?" CJ asked. "You're awful quiet."

"I'm always quiet," Bishop replied. His thoughts turned to the Manifold facility. He knew from experience that anything could be waiting for them—living, dead, reanimated or mechanical. He looked at CJ and wondered if the man had any idea what kind of shit might be waiting for them.

△ △ △

The desk clerk at the Evin was reluctant to talk until Massai offered him a few thousand rial. After that he told them everything they wanted to know. Not that the man had much information to offer. Yes, a man named Erik Somers had a reservation at the Evin. No, he hadn't checked in or called to cancel. No, he hadn't sent any luggage ahead. Yes, the room was still reserved for him.

That was all they could get. Even after a quick search of the room, they had nothing.

"What do we do now?" Ahmad asked.

Massai was just about to answer when his phone beeped. He pulled it out of his pocket, cast a worried look at Ahmad, and unfolded it.

"Massai, here… You have? Where is… Are you sure? Of course, I… Yes. Yes, we will do so right away." Massai closed the phone and stuck it back in his pocket.

"What was that about?" Ahmad asked.

"That was Shahid," he replied. "They found Somers. A traffic camera caught an image of him leaving Tehran on Freeway 7."

"Qom?"

"Unlikely. The camera also caught an image of the driver."

"What does that have to do with—"

"He is with *them*," Massai interrupted, emphasizing the last word. "The one called Joker was driving."

Ahmad winced. "Already? How did they know he was coming?"

"The same way we knew, I presume." Massai shook his head. His job had just gotten a lot more difficult. Still, there was one bright side to the latest news. "At least we know where they are going," he said.

Ahmad nodded. "We should hurry."

"Soon enough," Massai said. "But first we should go to the warehouse."

Ahmad nodded again.

The warehouse was where Massai's people stored their weapons. To get into the airport, it had been necessary to go in without a gun or even a knife. But if Somers was truly with Joker and his people, Massai and Ahmad would need to arm themselves before going after them.

Secretly, Massai was thrilled at the prospect of seeing Joker again. Nothing would make his day better than to put a bullet in that man's head.

6.

Hassi turned out to be more a gathering of houses than an actual village, at least that's what it looked like from the air. When CJ pointed to the speck on the horizon, Bishop at first thought he was pointing to a single building. As they grew closer, he spotted the individual structures that made up the village, including a rickety water tower and a squat, unadorned mosque. A few buildings he recognized as small businesses, but most of them looked like single-family houses, and many of those were spaced far apart. If there were more than five hundred people living in Hassi, he would be very surprised.

"What do these people do for work?" he asked.

"Most of them worked in the fields to the north," CJ replied. He pointed.

Bishop saw a huge swath of scorched earth sandwiched between the village and the foothills of the Alborz Mountains. Here and there, a few crops poked their way out of the soil, but most of the area looked burned and desolate.

"The jihadists," CJ said. "They came through and put just about everything to the torch."

Now Bishop saw the blackened squares of concrete between the houses. He hadn't noticed them before because the inhabitants had done a fair job of cleaning up, but now he recognized them as home foundations. The dark slabs of concrete were all that remained of houses that had been demolished.

"How many did they kill?"

"I'm not sure. Hassi had a population of about a thousand people a few months ago. Now, no more than a few hundred are left. Certainly there are no more than four hundred residents still living here."

"They killed six hundred people?"

"No, a lot of people fled when the jihadists came to town, but the bastards still managed to kill a couple hundred. Most of the people were simple farmers who tended the fields you saw." CJ shook his head; for once his ever-present smile was nowhere to be seen. "There won't be many crops to harvest this season. But even if there were, there's no one left to do it."

They landed the plane on a small road just to the east of Hassi. A battered green Saipa Z24 sat at the edge of the runway. A single occupant sat on the hood. The man looked to be in his sixties, or perhaps his seventies, with large, bushy white eyebrows and a few tufts of gray hair poking out from under his stained Red Sox cap. He waved to the plane and CJ brought it around.

"That's Ilias," CJ said. "An old friend of mine. He'll get us to the Manifold site."

"He has a truck," Bishop noted, pointing at the Saipa.

"It doesn't run. That thing's been sitting in that same spot for years."

Bishop looked again and noticed the flat, dry rotted tires, the large patches of rust and the smashed headlights. So much for a nice, easy drive to the site.

When the plane came to a stop, Bishop and CJ stepped out into the sunlight. The first thing Bishop noticed was the heat. Waves of it rolled upward from the sun-baked ground, making the image of the Saipa shimmer. Almost immediately, sweat began to pool in his underarms and on his forehead. Tehran had been warm, but the edge of the Kavir was *hot*.

CJ noticed his discomfort. "You were born here, weren't you? You'd think your body would be better prepared for this." He winked.

"I didn't complain," Bishop said.

"You get used to it, B. Just make sure you have enough water."

Bishop didn't need to be told. He'd spent plenty of time in arid regions on one mission or another. He knew how to get by. No Special Forces team ever went into service in the Middle East without some form of desert survival training; it was a prerequisite to deployment. As a Delta operative himself, CJ was undoubtedly aware of that.

He's probably just baiting me again, Bishop thought. He liked CJ, the man was easy with a smile and seemed perpetually cheerful. During his previous correspondence with the man, Bishop had never quite grasped the level of the man's geniality. Amazing how much of someone's character could get lost sending short, clipped messages through cyberspace. That said, he could do with a little less conversation and a little more action. "Let's get to it."

Ilias stood as they approached, his dry, cracked lips spreading into a wide gap-toothed grin.

"Welcome back, Hani," he said in Persian, embracing CJ. "It is good to see you."

"Hani?" Bishop asked.

CJ looked at him and for once managed to look a bit embarrassed. "It's a nickname. It means—"

"Happy," Bishop finished for him. "I know." The name fit CJ's personality.

CJ nodded. "Ilias is one of my oldest friends. He gave me the nickname as a child."

"I'll have to remember that one," Bishop said.

Ilias turned to Bishop and held out his hand, which Bishop took. "A pleasure to meet you," Ilias said in stilted English.

"Likewise," Bishop replied, then switched to Persian. "Where's our ride?"

"In a hurry?" Ilias asked.

"He's all business," CJ said. "I—"

"Actually," Bishop said. "We *are* in a hurry." They really didn't have time to share pleasantries. If this man really was a friend of CJ's, then he would get over the curt greeting.

"Of course," Ilias said with a nod, and motioned toward a copse of trees. "Apologies. Our transport is over there."

Bishop looked, and there, underneath the trees, were two small motorcycles with wide, fat tires, and a four-wheeler. The four-wheeler had a faded orange gas can and a blue cooler strapped to the rear rack. An old single shot rifle was secured to the front rack. Bishop recognized the bikes as Yamaha Big Wheels, which were popular back in the late eighties, along with big hair and parachute pants. But the wide, knobby tires would be perfect for riding through the desert.

Seeing the rifle strapped to the four-wheeler reminded him that he hadn't secured a weapon yet. He turned to CJ. "Have something with a trigger and bullets for me?"

"Of course," CJ said. He turned back to the plane and stuck his head into the cabin. After a few minutes rooting around behind the passenger seats, he produced a large black suitcase and a pair of green, military-style backpacks. "One of the benefits of flying an ugly, beat up plane," he said. "No one ever bothers to search it." He set the suitcase and the packs on the ground and opened the case, showing Bishop the contents.

Inside were four pistols. A Desert Eagle .357, two Sig Sauer P220, and a matte, black Beretta .380 Cheetah with an improvised laser sight. Beside each gun was a pair of extra clips, all loaded. CJ reached in and grabbed the Beretta, then tucked it into the rear waistband of his pants.

"This one's mine," he said. He grabbed the two clips and put them in his front pocket.

Bishop looked at the suitcase. He grabbed one of the Sigs, checked the safety, and tucked it into his waistband. Then he grabbed the two extra clips, along with the two clips from the second Sig, and shoved all four into his pockets.

"Think you'll need that much ammunition?" CJ asked.

"You're aware of the kind of weapon I normally carry?" Bishop said.

CJ laughed and closed the suitcase. Bishop was well known for carrying large, chain-fed machine guns that could level an army. The Sigs were pellet guns in comparison. "Fair enough," CJ said, then put the suitcase back on the plane. He handed one of the backpacks to Bishop and slung the second over his shoulder.

"Pretty standard stuff in there," CJ said. "Canteen, matches, MREs, that sort of thing. Plenty of room for more if you need any samples."

Bishop nodded, then put his arms through the straps.

"What about Ilias?" he asked.

"He's got his rifle. That's all he needs. Right Ilias?"

Ilias nodded, then showed Bishop his right hand. It shook with a mild palsy, and Bishop understood. The old man would never be able to aim a pistol properly, but he could brace a rifle against something—a four-wheeler, perhaps—and still be an effective shot. Although it limited his availability in a crisis. Still, looking at Ilias with his wrinkled skin and rheumy eyes, Bishop wasn't sure how much use the old man would be in a firefight, anyway.

"All right, then," Bishop said, swinging a leg over one of the bikes. "Let's go."

Together, the three men sped south over the dry, unforgiving terrain.

△ △ △

Massai and Ahmad sat in the rear of the Bell 206 LongRanger, while the pilot—a grumpy, middle aged Iraqi refugee named Devan—flew on in silence. The two men had been forced by limited aircraft and time constraints to secure a private aircraft for this trip, and Devan had been the first available pilot they found. They'd interrupted his lunch, and he complained loudly about it until Massai, in a moment of weakness, had allowed the man to see his pistol. After that, the pilot wisely kept quiet.

It was all a bluff. Massai couldn't harm the man. Neither he nor Ahmad knew how to fly a helicopter, and they were flying over the desert. Even after they landed, they would still need to get back. Hopefully they would have Somers with them when they did.

The desert passed below the blue and tan charter helicopter at a rapid pace, but to Massai it seemed they were barely moving. Joker and Somers could already be there, and who knew what reinforcements they could have accumulated in the interim? Probably none yet, but CJ would find allies soon enough, and Massai had only Ahmad and a reluctant, grumpy pilot.

He leaned forward and poked his head between the two front seats. "Is this the fastest you can go?" he asked.

"We are already traveling at 220 kilometers per hour," Devan replied.

"Can we go faster?"

"I am sorry, but this is as fast as the helicopter goes."

Massai grunted, then sat back in his seat. "220 kilometers per hour. They are probably in Joker's plane already, and they have a large head start. We should have waited for the Sikorsky." Shahid's sleek black Sikorsky S70—the civilian version of the famed Blackhawk—could fly at speeds of over 350 kp/h. They would have had no trouble catching up to Joker and Somers in that, but there was no time to get it here. Shahid had promised to send it to Hassi as soon as he could, along with the pilot and the mounted minigun, which would have proven very useful if Joker had any of his friends with him.

Ahmad put his hand on his partner's shoulder. "Allah is watching over us. You will see. Even if they are in Joker's plane, it does not go any faster than this helicopter, and he cannot land it in the Kavir, so they will have to travel overland from Hassi. We *can* land in the Kavir. The advantage is still ours."

Massai tried to share Ahmad's fervor, but he had never been as spiritual as some of his countrymen. He tried to think of his lack of faith as realism. Too often, his comrades would rely solely on the will of Allah to get them through any tough situation, and all too often, it ended with someone dying. His friends and associates would attribute this to "Allah's will" and go on as if that solved everything, but Massai's pragmatic side would remind him that he could do better for himself and his people by staying alive as long as possible. It wasn't that he didn't have any faith at all, Massai simply preferred to try to keep himself safe and let Allah worry about bigger things, like running the universe.

"How long before we reach the site?" he asked, raising his voice to make sure Devan heard him from the back seat.

"The coordinates you gave me are not far," Devan replied. "As long as they are correct, we will be there within an hour."

As long as they are correct, Massai mused. The pilot was finding his courage again. He briefly entertained the notion of putting the fear of death back into Devan, but decided against it. When they reached the site, they might need all the courage they could get.

7.

The ride to the site didn't take very long. What had taken the two men from Hassi that had inadvertently discovered the site, a day and a half to walk, took less than three hours on the bikes. Sometime around sixteen hundred hours, Bishop pulled his bike to a stop alongside a large concrete cylinder sticking up from the ground. Atop the cylinder was a solar panel ten feet long and half as tall. Not nearly enough of a panel to power any sizable outpost, even with the constant sunshine of the Kavir Desert to charge it, at least under normal circumstances.

But nothing about Manifold ever turned out to be normal. Ridley had already impressed everyone from physicists to guys with a PhD in engineering with some of his advanced technology. This would probably prove to be more of the same. Bishop made a mental note to take pictures of anything that looked like it might be useful intel, as he got off the bike and stretched.

"Still clear?" CJ's voice crackled through the radio on his waist. Bishop grabbed it and brought it up to his face.

"Clear," he said.

"On our way," CJ replied. He and Ilias were about a hundred yards back, watching through field glasses. They had stopped at that distance to assess the approachability of the outpost. After watching through the binoculars for about half an hour, they'd had a short debate over who should make the initial approach. It ended when Bishop crossed his arms and looked down at his temporary partner whose thigh was about the same thickness as Bishop's upper arm.

Bishop had approached with one hand on the throttle and the other on his pistol, fully expecting to be accosted by guards before he reached his destination. But nothing happened.

He heard CJ's bike rev, and a few minutes later, they stood side by side looking up at the top of the cylinder. Ilias had remained behind, his rifle now mounted to a little tripod on the front of his four-wheeler. He would cover them if things went bad in a hurry.

"How good is he with that rifle?" Bishop asked.

"Pretty damn good," CJ replied. "He might not look like much, but that old geezer is a product of the Iranian Special Forces. They forced him out after they discovered his palsy a few years ago, and he came to Hassi to live a quiet, nonmilitary life. But he's still got the eye. As long as the rifle is braced against something solid, he could shoot the tail off a field mouse at five hundred yards."

"Field mice don't shoot back," Bishop said, but even inaccurate cover was better than no cover. He turned his attention back to the cylinder and resumed his examination of the site's exterior. There were no cameras or security devices that he could see. The only wires that ran into the structure came from the solar panel. In fact, the only other feature on the outside was a vertical set of metal bars that formed a crude ladder to the top. Since he couldn't find any way in, he reasoned that the door must be on top of the cylinder.

"I guess we go up," CJ said, echoing Bishop's thoughts.

Bishop went first, climbing the ladder and pulling himself up and over the edge in less than two seconds. Once at the top, he noted the hatch. It should pull right up, provided it wasn't locked. But what would he find when he opened it? An empty site? Or a small army of heavily armed terrorists? He turned toward Ilias and saw the man staring at him through the scope of his rifle.

CJ pulled himself up next to Bishop and casually reached out to open the hatch. Bishop grabbed his arm, stopping him. *It's a wonder the man is still alive*, Bishop thought. *He's as quick to act, as he is to talk.* "Slow down."

"Nobody's home, B."

Bishop agreed with the man. There were no guards. No fresh tracks. But that didn't mean there wouldn't be any danger. Tracks could be concealed, as could security measures, not to mention traps. And Manifold was good at all of the above. "Pull the hatch on three. I'll sweep."

"Roger," CJ said. He took his place at the side of the hatch. He crouched and took hold of the hatch's handle. "Ready," he said.

Bishop aimed his Sig toward the still closed hatch. If he saw anything move inside, it would get a bullet. Or three. "One."

CJ tightened his grip on the hatch.

"Two…three!"

CJ jerked the door upward.

Bishop began to lean over the hole, sweeping the Sig from right to left. As he did, he saw the familiar shape of a shotgun barrel just a foot below. But instead of firing he flinched back, yanking his arms away from the opening.

The shotgun boomed just as the hatch fully opened and a fraction of a second before Bishop pulled his arm back. There was a pinch of pain in his forearm but he ignored it when he saw CJ spill over the side.

8.

"Damn!" Bishop swore, skirting the now open hatch. With his free hand, he grabbed his radio. "Ilias, CJ is down. Repeat, CJ is down. Can you—"

A string of coughs and curses rose up from the other side of the cylinder. "I'm okay," CJ said. "—the hell happened?"

Bishop looked back to the hatch. He could see the unmoving shotgun muzzle. "A trap." He'd seen the shotgun with no operator when the hatch opened. It wasn't exactly a deterrent to any force larger than two, but it could have killed one of them.

CJ popped back up over the edge of the roof.

"You hit?" Bishop asked.

"No. I tripped." CJ held up a finger and was clearly about to defend himself, but looked suddenly serious. He turned the extended finger toward Bishop's left arm. "But you were hit."

Bishop looked at the arm. The sleeve was stained with blood. Not a lot, but enough. He rolled up his sleeve. The blood came from a small red hole where a single ball of buckshot had struck. He saw the lump of metal just beneath his skin, a centimeter away from the wound. He pushed his thumb against the ball of metal and pushed it back toward the wound.

CJ sucked in a quick breath. "Geez."

The black ball popped out of the wound a moment later. Bishop picked it up, rolled it between his fingers and flicked it away.

"That's…hardcore, B."

Bishop leaned slowly over the open hatch, aiming his Sig down the hole. He saw no movement and the shotgun had been spent. It was a trap using a system of wires and pulleys, rigged to fire when the hatch was opened. Not likely to be the work of Manifold. Too crude.

"You going to take care of that?" CJ asked, motioning to the wound.

"It'll stop on its own," Bishop said. "I'm on point."

CJ nodded. For once, it seemed, he was out of bravado.

Bishop checked the trap once more to make sure it couldn't fire again. The shotgun was old, but clearly still functional. However, it had been loaded for just one shot. Without someone to pull the trigger a second time, it was technically disarmed. That didn't stop him from kicking apart the wire and pulley system. With the trap in ruins, he put his pistol in his waistband and grabbed the top rung of the inside ladder.

"Cover me," he said.

CJ nodded and pointed his Beretta down into the building. "If anyone pokes their head out, I'll put a bullet in it."

Bishop lowered himself down into the structure. CJ would come down behind him. So far, the guy had proven pretty handy, if only he'd take this a little more seriously. He reminded Bishop of Rook in that sense.

Thinking of Rook brought a twinge of tension to his back. The team hadn't heard from him since they lost contact with him in the former Soviet Union. He had yet to resurface. Bishop hoped his friend was all right. Too often, someone on the team would say something, and then pause for Rook's inevitable jab, but it never came. It was weird, like losing a limb. It felt like it was there, and it *should* be there, but no matter how many times you closed your eyes and opened them again, it never grew back. Queen took Rook's disappearance the hardest. She hadn't said much to anyone before heading out on a personal mission to find him, but it was obvious to everyone how heavily his disappearance weighed on her mind.

Rook will be fine, he thought. *He can take care of himself.* Bishop found himself wondering what Queen would do first when Rook finally did resurface. She'd most likely either hit him or kiss him. Probably both.

He reached the bottom of the ladder and looked around, squeezing thoughts of Rook and Queen from his mind. The last thing he needed right now was to be distracted. He would worry about his friends when this ergot business was finished.

He stood in the center of a large room filled with computers and other electronics. Everywhere he looked, a light blinked or a control screen beeped. Here and there, he spotted signs of human habitation: a coffee cup, an empty water bottle, a jacket draped over a chair. Yet there was not a single person in sight, and a thin layer of dust coated everything in the room.

Almost everything, he realized when he looked down.

Multiple sets of footprints marred the dust on the floor. The tracks led in every direction, and occasionally he spotted a square of dust-free space that he guessed to be the former location of lab equipment. Someone had gone through the place and taken everything they deemed valuable. Bishop's money was on the jihadists. They hadn't taken much, though. They probably didn't know how to use most of it. Bishop could relate. The vast array of blinking and beeping machines would confuse just about anyone who wasn't trained in their use. The only thing he thought he recognized was a base unit for a small, hardwired security system. If he followed the wires leading out of the unit, they would probably take him right to the facility's security console. He would have to check that out before he left; there might be some video files that would help.

"All clear?" CJ asked from the entrance above.

"Clear," Bishop replied, moving deeper into the facility, following some tracks.

He walked down a narrow hallway, passing numerous doors that opened into empty rooms. Tracks leading in and out of the rooms indicated that the jihadists had looted most of them, but as he looked into one room, he found a plain white refrigerator in a corner. The door hung open, facing him and blocking his view of the inside. On the door was a bright yellow and black Biohazard sign.

"Uh-oh," CJ said behind him. "Don't get too close."

Bishop ignored him and took a step forward. He walked around the refrigerator, giving it a healthy distance, and peered inside.

It was empty.

"They took whatever was in there," he said.

"They got the weaponized ergot?" CJ asked.

Bishop shook his head, just how much *did* CJ know, anyway? He would have to have a long talk with Deep Blue and Keasling when he got back. "Looks like it."

"This is bad," CJ said.

"Keep looking. Maybe we'll find something useful."

The room with the refrigerator occupied a corner of the facility, with the hallway leading off in two directions. They split up, with Bishop going right and CJ going left. Numerous doors lined Bishop's section of hallway, but none of them were locked. Some had been forced open by a crowbar or some other tool. All proved useless. The very last door opened up on a room lined with row upon row of empty shelves. Bishop tried to think of what it could have been used for when he spotted the empty potato chip wrappers in the corner.

Food storage, he realized. It had been cleaned out, as well. No surprise, there. He turned and walked out of the room, almost bumping into CJ. He dodged aside just in time to avoid crashing into the man. Why was he back already? Had he found something? Had he even looked?

"That was fast," Bishop said.

"Sorry, B," CJ said. "I should have warned you I was there."

"Did you find anything?" Bishop said, ignoring the apology.

"As a matter of fact, I did. That's why I was coming to get you. Follow me."

CJ turned and walked back the way he'd come. Bishop fell into step behind him, wondering what was so important CJ couldn't just tell him what he'd found. When they reached the other end of the hall CJ opened a door on the right. Judging by the icon painted on the front of the door, he was leading Bishop into the facility's lavatory.

Bishop stepped into the room and stopped. Not everyone had left the facility, it seemed.

Two dead men sat on the floor in a rust-colored puddle of dried blood, propped next to one of the urinals. The bodies leaned against the wall in a sitting position on either side of a urinal. Both looked to be of Arab descent, with black hair and dark, Mediterranean skin that had paled somewhat after their deaths.

The cause of death for each was immediately obvious. One of the men had a flat spot on the back of his head where his skull had been caved in, and the other sported a single gunshot wound to the head. The dry air and moderate temperature had combined to preserve the bodies a bit, but decomposition had begun, and the room smelled of dead flesh.

"That's nasty," CJ said. "What kind of guy wants to take a leak with that right next to him?"

Bishop ignored the joke. There was nothing funny about this. "Any idea who they might be?"

"A couple of terrorists who pissed off the rest of the bunch?" CJ offered.

"Maybe," Bishop said. "But weren't there two guys from Hassi that led the terrorists here by mistake?"

"You think that's who these two are?"

"It's as good a theory as any. And I know how we can find out."

"How?"

"I think this place had security cameras inside. I've noticed a bunch of wires close to the ceiling that look like they've been snipped. If we find the room where their security was based, maybe we can scan the video files. That should tell us something."

CJ's eyes widened. "That's a pretty good idea. But what if they took the security system?"

"I don't think they did," Bishop said. "They might have taken the cameras, but I think the system itself is still here."

"You saw it, already. Didn't you?"

Bishop nodded. "Just the base unit. Back in that first room. If we follow those wires," he pointed to the ceiling, where a group of cables ran along the length of the wall, "we should be able to find it."

"You're good," CJ said, his smile returned. "Let's do it."

The two followed the wires to a room in the center of the facility. The door was solid steel with a large window made from reinforced glass. The door stood ajar, and Bishop pulled the handle to reveal a small room with a bank of monitors on the front wall. There were eight monitors in all, and each one flashed static, casting the room in an eerie light. On the left hand wall was an empty rifle rack, and on the right wall was a row of cabinets. All the doors were open, showing them to be empty. Here and there a stray round sat on floor, the brass casings glinting in the light of the monitors, and Bishop guessed the cabinets to have been used for ammunition, among other things. The jihadists had even taken the chairs.

"They really cleaned this place out," CJ said.

Bishop stepped into the room. He walked over to the bank of monitors and examined them. The equipment had been left intact. The terrorists probably hadn't seen a need to smash it since no one knew the place existed, but had they searched it thoroughly? He hoped not. In less than a minute, he found what he was looking for.

"There it is," he said. He reached into his backpack and pulled out the KA-BAR knife CJ had supplied, which he then inserted into a thin seam in the base of the bank of monitors. After a few moments of prying, a panel popped off, revealing a compartment underneath. The door to the compartment was locked, but the designer hadn't put in a very strong lock. Most likely, they didn't think they would need one since the compartment itself was supposed to be hidden.

"Did I say you were good?" CJ asked. "You're James Freaking Bond."

Bishop didn't reply. Instead, he jammed the KA-BAR into the compartment seam and pried it open. It took a few seconds, but the lock eventually gave under the pressure and the compartment popped open, revealing a stack of DVDs. Bishop looked through the discs; all of them were labeled according to date and sector, with the last of the entries dated just over two weeks previous. Above the compartment, a single DVD drive sat, its light blinking red. Bishop touched the eject button and another DVD came out. This one was dated the day the two men from Hassi had found the place. He held it up to show CJ.

"Score!" CJ said, and held up his palm for a high five.

Bishop looked at CJ's upraised hand and raised a single eyebrow in response. Not a chance. "These should tell us everything we need to know about who raided this place."

CJ lowered his hand. "Here…" He reached around his back and removed his backpack. "Stick 'em in there for the time being. We can watch them when we get back to Hassi."

"We might be able to watch them now," Bishop offered. "If the technicians were living here, there's bound to be a DVD player somewhere."

"Unless the terrorists stole it," CJ said. "Those guys like to watch movies too, you know."

"It won't hurt to look. Besides, we—"

"You guys should get out of there," Ilias's voice crackled through the radio. "There is a helicopter coming. I can see it without my rifle scope. Ten kilometers away. Perhaps less, and moving fast."

"Is it one of ours?" CJ asked into the radio.

"No, it looks like a charter. I can't read the writing from here, but it has two-tone paint. Blue and tan, and it is flying straight toward us. No question. This is its destination."

Bishop shoved the DVDs into CJ's pack. "Let's move."

"You don't have to tell me twice," CJ replied, and both men ran for the exit.

On the way out, Bishop's foot kicked something. He turned just in time to see a clear water bottle roll across the floor. It sported a bright yellow biohazard symbol on the label. The jihadists must have missed it. He thought he should grab a sample for the lab back in the US.

Bishop paused for a moment to pick up the bottle and look at it. The liquid inside was perfectly clear, and could easily be mistaken for water. In fact, it probably *was* water. Water infected with Manifold's new and improved ergot. If someone were to drink it, say, someone who didn't know what the biohazard symbol meant, they would be in for a nasty shock.

"You coming, B?" CJ shouted from the exit.

"Right behind you," he replied. He shoved the bottle into his pack and ran to the ladder. When he reached the top, CJ was waiting for him.

"What kept you?" CJ asked.

"Later," Bishop said. "Where is that chopper?"

"Right there," CJ pointed.

Ilias was wrong. The helicopter wasn't ten kilometers out. It was hovering right over their bikes.

△ △ △

Ilias squatted behind the four wheeler, his eye glued to the scope. He could make out the pilot's head through the helicopter's portside window. So far, they hadn't paid him very much attention. He was just an old man, after all. They wouldn't be the first people to underestimate him, and probably not the last, either. He lined up the scope and looked for a reference to judge the wind. The backwash from the helicopter made a wind check impossible, however. He would have to wing it.

So be it.

He lined up the scope again, putting the pilot's head right in his crosshairs, and his finger pressed down on the trigger.

△ △ △

It all happened in a matter of seconds, but to Massai the time slowed to a crawl. The first bullet pinged into the cockpit from behind and exited the windshield only slightly to the left of Devan's head. Massai immediately opened the aircraft's portside door and returned fire with his pistol, a Sig 1911. After his first few shots, the bullets seemed to come from everywhere at once.

Devan screamed, while Ahmad opened the door on the other side and propped his rifle against the seat. Massai didn't have time to watch him, but he knew Ahmad would take his time and aim well. He was as good with that rifle as anyone. If Massai could cover him on this side, Ahmad could make a shot that counted.

The sound of shots mixed with the ping of bullets as they tore through the interior of the helicopter, but Massai kept his eyes on the two men taking cover behind the old Manifold facility. They worked in tandem; one would pop out and fire off a few rounds while the other hid behind the concrete cylinder, then they would switch. Massai found himself hiding behind the helicopter's doorframe more often than not, but he managed to keep up a steady stream of return fire, even if he wasn't able to aim for each shot.

Because of their tactics, his opponents had more time to aim. Their shots clattered around the interior of the helicopter with an accuracy that Massai feared would prove too much to overcome. Eventually someone inside the helicopter would get hit, or a bullet would pierce the gas tank, and that would be it.

Behind him, Ahmad's rifle boomed. Even with the sound of gunshots all around, the rifle sounded like a cannon in the confines of the Bell 206.

"The man by the four-wheeler is down," Ahmad said.

Massai barely heard him over the ringing in his ears.

"Good," Massai said. "That just leaves Somers and The Joker."

"Pull us around," Ahmad said to Devan. "Take us around the cylinder so we can get a better shot."

"Are you insane?" Devan shouted. "They are shooting at us."

"And we are shooting at them," Massai said. "Let us hope we are better shots than they are."

"What if you aren't?" Devan asked.

"Then I hope you are ready to meet Allah," Ahmad said.

△ △ △

Bishop stepped out from behind the cylinder and took another shot, sending several rounds through the windshield of the helicopter but not scoring any hits to the pilot or either of the gunmen, who must have been reloading because they did not shoot back.

As soon as he ducked back behind the concrete, shots rang out again, and after a moment he heard CJ's grunt of pain.

"Damn!" CJ said. "The guy with the rifle is good!"

"You hurt bad?" Bishop asked.

"Just a scratch."

"We need to move," Bishop said. "Sooner or later they are going to fly that thing around the concrete and try to get us from a different angle. Draw their fire. I'll get to the bikes."

"*Draw their fire?*" CJ said, sounding aghast. "What the hell do you think—" A shot rang out and sent him ducking. The concrete just above his head exploded as a high caliber round struck home. Had the bullet found its target, CJ's head would have been reduced to gore.

Bishop sprinted out from behind the cylinder and made a beeline for the Big Wheel. Behind him, CJ shouted at the helicopter and started firing. Almost immediately, shots rang out from the chopper. Bishop waited for the sand at his feet to erupt with slugs as they tried to cut him down. He reminded himself that he couldn't regenerate if he got shot, so he made sure to run in a random zigzag pattern, ducking into a roll every now and then to throw off the shooter's aim.

But the shots never came.

When he reached the bike, he risked a look back at the helicopter. The shooters seemed to be concentrating on CJ. He climbed on the bike and pulled out his pistol. Most people couldn't ride and shoot at the same time, because the throttle is on the right. But he'd been trained by Delta and could shoot just as well with both hands.

He revved the engine and took off toward the chopper as they spun away from him in pursuit of CJ, who was dodging the helicopter the same way kids have a standoff on either side of a kitchen table—by running around and around. But eventually someone figures out that they can go under the table. Or in this case, over the table. CJ didn't have long.

Bishop fired several rounds, but they ricocheted harmlessly off the helicopter's fuselage. 9mm rounds were designed to punch through flesh, not thick metal. He'd have to get up close and personal. Luckily, the sound of the chopper drowned out the sound of his ride and shots. They might have seen him run, but they had no idea he was coming back.

Moving as fast as he could, Bishop steered the Big Wheel around in an arc, moving closer, but keeping behind the chopper' tail. As the helicopter rounded the concrete cylinder, it came lower to the ground, hovering just twenty feet up. It was a dangerous place for them to be, but the rotor backwash was kicking up so much dust, CJ would be blinded.

They were moving in for the kill.

So was Bishop.

He cut his angle of approach, aiming for the helicopter as it spun, and the large rock below it. He would reach the chopper just as the pilot turned its side to him. What he was about to attempt wasn't his style. It was more Queen's M.O., but he'd seen her in action enough to wing it. As the bike sped up, the chopper spun around and descended a few more feet.

Just right, Bishop thought. Too high and he'd miss. Too low and he'd get sliced to bits by the rotor blades. After a quick adjustment to his course, Bishop got his feet up beneath him, and crouched, keeping the throttle wide open.

Then, the Big Wheel crashed.

The large rock was just the tip of something even bigger, buried beneath the desert. It stopped the vehicle in its tracks, launching the back end up. Bishop pushed off the seat at the same time catapulting into the air. The man with the rifle didn't see him coming until the last minute, but he flinched away in time to dodge Bishop's first shot.

He never got to take a second. His arc through the air brought him below the helicopter. But not too low. Bishop collided with the helicopter's skids and wrapped his arms around it. The helicopter pitched to the side, because the pilot was not prepared for the sudden weight change. Bishop's body ached, but he fought to hold on. The helicopter nearly crashed, but the pilot managed to right the craft. When he did, Bishop pulled himself up to the open door. He couldn't see well because his eyes were watering from the helicopter wash, but he had to try.

Holding onto the skids with just his legs, Bishop unloaded his clip into the cockpit. When the gun clicked empty, he let go. The ground greeted him harshly, knocking the air from his lungs, but the fall had been short—just eight feet. While he caught his breath, he quickly reloaded the Sig and took aim at the helicopter again. He didn't fire. He just waited.

But the helicopter didn't swing around.

△ △ △

Devan screamed, but Massai barely heard it over the sound of rotors. He risked a look over at the pilot and saw a large red stain on Devan's left shoulder, the one closest to the window. The stain bloomed outward in an ever-expanding flow, and Massai knew they could not keep this up.

"Swing around!" Ahmad said.

"It's too late," Massai replied. "Devan is hit."

Devan slumped into the seat, his right hand clutching the stick while his left shoulder pumped blood freely through his shirt. Massai was impressed. Most men would have grabbed the wound and tried to staunch the bleeding, but Devan kept enough presence of mind to keep flying despite the pain. Of course, by the look on the Iraqi's face, it could be simple shock.

"Devan," Massai shouted, "You have to land. Now."

"Land? Here? Are you crazy? Did you see what that man just did? I'm getting out of here as fast as I can go." The aircraft pitched to the side as Devan made a hasty u-turn.

"You are losing too much blood, Devan," Massai said.

"Those men have already shot me once," Devan said. "I will not give them a chance to do it again."

If either of them had known how to fly a helicopter, Massai would have yanked Devan from the pilot's seat and taken control, but as it was, they had to watch their pilot as the shock and adrenaline started to wear off. Massai tried his best to staunch the flow of blood, but the angle was bad and Devan squirmed and writhed in the seat. At least he flew low over the ground, though that would not matter much at 220 kp/h.

Less than three minutes after the first shot was fired, Devan's eyes began to droop. Thirty seconds after, he lost consciousness altogether. Massai and Ahmad watched helplessly as the desert floor rose up to meet them.

9.

Bishop watched the helicopter fly west, toward Qom, until it simply fell out of the sky. He did not see the chopper crash, but from the last few erratic moments of its flight, he was sure it had. There was no explosion—those usually only happened in Hollywood, but a few seconds later he heard a distant sound that was most likely the helicopter hitting the sand. Bishop guessed the crash site to be no more than two or three kilometers distant.

CJ poked his head from behind the concrete, then seeing that the coast was clear, he came running up to Bishop. The sleeve just above his right elbow was red with blood, but he looked otherwise unhurt.

"Everything functional?" Bishop asked.

"That was, ahh, that was some really crazy shit there, B."

Bishop grinned. "Yes. It was. Now are you okay?"

CJ nodded, flexing his arm to show he was fine. "Bastards shot my backpack, though. Blew a hole right through my canteen and bent the blade of my KA-BAR."

"The DVDs?"

CJ shook his head. "K.I.A."

Damn. Those DVDs were important.

"Should we investigate the chopper?" CJ asked.

Bishop shook his head, no. "Check on Ilias."

Ilias was dead, killed by a single shot through the chest. The wound looked to be the work of a large caliber rifle. Probably a .50 cal with a scope, judging by the size of the exit wound and the single loud shot that had come from the helicopter. They wouldn't know unless they searched for the bullet, but something told Bishop they didn't have time.

"Did you get a look at any of them?" CJ asked.

Bishop shook his head. He'd seen the rifleman as he flew through the air, but it was just a glimpse, and he was more focused on not being sliced into bits, shot or bludgeoned by the helicopter at the time.

"You?"

"Just the pilot."

"He look familiar?"

"Unfortunately, yes," CJ replied. "He works for your father's group."

"My father? This is his doing?"

"Looks that way."

Bishop looked out at the cylinder and imagined the two men dead within. Then he looked over at Ilias, whose blood continued to soak into the dry desert soil. He shouldn't be surprised. CJ had told him Dawoud Abbasi was a terrorist, after all, but still. It bothered him to think he could be related to such a man.

It would explain why Ilias had been the first to shoot, too. Ordinarily, operatives were not supposed to engage an unidentified party unless the party engaged them first. But if Ilias had recognized the men as terrorists, that would be different. In such cases, shooting first was widely accepted as a proper course of action.

"We should get out of here," CJ said. "If those guys knew we were here, more are probably on their way." He looked at the Big Wheel. The front end was crumpled in where it had struck the rock. It might run, but Bishop didn't want to rely on the beaten machine. "I'll take Ilias's ride. You take the other."

Bishop looked at the dead man's body. There wasn't time to bury the man or even take his body with them. Fresh anger welled within him. Somehow, someone was going to pay for the old man's death. It felt good to let the anger in. Like inviting an old friend to dinner. He and it had a lot of catching up to do, and they could start on the ride back to Hassi.

"Let's go," CJ said. He slid Ilias off the ATV, wiped off as much blood as he could and started the engine.

Bishop followed suit, swinging his leg over the Big Wheel. He said a mental goodbye to Ilias and started the bike, then he and CJ rode away from the Manifold facility, headed for Hassi. From there, they would take CJ's plane to Shiraz, where Bishop would finally meet his father.

He thought of the Sig in his waistband and realized the meeting would not be the friendly one he'd first imagined.

△ △ △

Just before the impact, Massai grabbed the stick from Devan's limp hand and pulled it back. It was the only thing he could think to do. The craft tilted upward and slowed, and for a moment he thought it would be like flying a small plane, but then the stick jerked to the right and the whole craft pitched sideways. The stick bucked and jerked like a living thing, and soon ripped itself free of his grip. The Bell spun and rolled its way to the desert floor while he tried to get into his seat. Just before he could buckle himself in, they hit the ground with an ear splitting metallic screech. Then the whole world turned into a bright white light.

The next thing he knew, he was lying on his back. He looked up to see the cockpit of the Bell above him. Devan hung upside down from his seat, his broken body still strapped into the pilot's seat. Blood dripped from the wound in his shoulder to patter onto the vinyl of the seat next to Massai. By the angle of Devan's head, there was no way the pilot could still be alive. Massai checked for a pulse anyway, just be sure, and found none.

He glanced at the radio. It looked fine. At least there was that.

"Ahmad," he called. "Are you there?"

"I am here," Ahmad said from somewhere outside the wreckage. "Are you hurt?"

"Not badly," Massai replied. His head ached, and he felt a warm trickle from his right temple to his jaw that could only be blood. His left wrist stung, leading him to believe he'd sprained it, and two of his ribs felt like they might be broken. But it could have been much worse. Both his legs worked, and that was the main thing. It meant he could walk. "How about you?"

"I am fine. A few scratches, nothing more." Massai couldn't believe it. He pulled himself out of the wreckage to find Ahmad kneeling in the sand about five feet away and praying. He didn't have his mat with him, but he didn't seem to mind putting his knees in the dirt and prostrating himself on the desert floor. After a few minutes of prayer, he stood up, brushed the sand off his knees, and smiled.

"The radio looks all right," Massai offered.

Ahmad's smile grew. "I told you Allah would protect us," he said cheerfully.

Massai would have preferred Allah be a bit more proactive in his protection, but he kept that thought to himself. "Devan is dead."

Ahmad didn't flinch. Death was nothing new to either of them.

Massai noted several tracks around the helicopter, including a set that went away from the crash and then returned. "How long was I unconscious?"

"Twenty minutes. I used that time to look around."

"Do you know where we are?"

"A few kilometers west of the research facility."

"You saw it?"

Ahmad produced a pair of binoculars from the ground at his feet and handed them to Massai. "If you climb over that small ridge, you can see for yourself."

Massai took the binoculars but didn't bother to look. "Are they still there?"

"No, they have long gone, but they left one of the motorcycles behind."

"Do you think Joker disabled it?"

"It looks good from here," Ahmad answered. "In any case, it is a better alternative to the radio."

Massai couldn't argue. He could probably raise Shahid on the radio, but there was never any telling who might be listening. It would be better to take the bike and ride it back to Hassi. Once there he could contact Shahid on an encrypted line, as long as his cell phone still worked.

He pulled it out of his pocket and turned it on. As he suspected, he had no signal at all, but at least it was still working. He turned it off to save the battery and started walking.

An hour later, he and Ahmad, sweating and cursing, reached the concrete cylinder that marked the entrance to manifold's facility. By then, both men were parched and thirsty, but there was no water to be had anywhere. Joker and Somers had taken the four-wheeler he'd seen earlier, and thus the cooler and gas it carried. He'd expected as much, of course.

Ahmad examined the Yamaha, checking the fuel level of the tank, and nodded. "Nearly full," he said. The front end looked bent, but the engine seemed intact.

Good. The ride might not be comfortable, but it should get them back to Hassi. From there they would call in the Sikorsky.

"They will still beat us there," Ahmad said. "They have too great a head start."

Massai nodded. "But we know where they are going."

"Shiraz," Ahmad said.

Massai nodded. "We will confront them there, in the Abbasi…what is that?"

In the dirt by the cylinder, Massai spotted a crumpled green shape. He walked over to it and recognized it as a backpack. Olive green, not quite military issue, but clearly modeled after those given out by the Iranian Army. On the flap was a sewn-on patch featuring The Joker from the American comic books.

"It's his," Ahmad said.

Massai picked it up and looked inside. He couldn't believe his luck. In addition to four bottles of water, the pack had ammunition for a .380 pistol, several packs of American MREs, a knife, a flashlight and ten or twelve DVDs. He picked up one of the DVDs and read the writing on the disk.

Manifold, Ergot Facility, Camera 12 - April 14, 2010. 1600 to 0000.

Security tapes from inside the facility!

"What are these doing out here?" he wondered aloud.

"The Joker must have been taking them and dropped his pack during the fight."

"Why would he want them?"

"I do not know," Ahmad said. "Perhaps it was Somers who grabbed them."

That made more sense. Massai could see why Somers would want to view the DVDs, but there was nothing on them that CJ did not already know.

Ahmad grabbed one of the bottled waters and took a long drink. "Still cool," he said. "I told you, Massai."

"I know," Massai said. "Allah is watching over us." He took one of the bottles and brought it to his lips. The cool, clean water rolled down his throat, cooling his entire body.

"Praise Allah," Ahmad said.

This time, Massai joined him.

10.

Bishop watched the land below as it rolled out underneath them. They had left Hassi in CJ's Cessna several hours ago and were well on their way to Shiraz. Both men had eaten a light supper in the small village prior to boarding the Cessna, but Bishop found he didn't have much appetite. Not only was he about to meet his biological father for the first time, he was going to have to arrest him.

Maybe kill him.

"I still can't believe we lost the security DVDs," he said. "We could have used them to confirm Abbasi's involvement."

"We don't need them," CJ replied. "I saw the pilot. I know the guy. He was your father's—"

"Abbasi's," Bishop corrected.

"Abbasi's man," CJ finished.

Bishop nodded. Blood or no blood, his father was Darren Somers from eastern Illinois. This Dawoud Abbasi guy was just another terrorist, as far as he was concerned. He checked the pistol in his waistband for the tenth time since he'd gotten in the plane.

CJ laughed. "Is it still loaded since the last time you checked?"

Bishop didn't respond. He hadn't used any of his meditative techniques to stem the growing coal of anger in his belly, and the longer he waited—and the more he thought about the old man's death—the greater the pressure building inside him. He sat in silence, willing the Cessna to go faster. He knew a Cessna 172 was capable of speeds up to 180 miles per hour, but it was dangerous to fly them that fast. They simply weren't built to handle that much stress. The cruising speed of a typical 172 was somewhere around 140 mph. By Bishop's estimation, they were traveling a little over 140, so he couldn't push CJ to add throttle. He would just have to be patient for a while longer. They would get there when they got there.

And when we do, I'm going to have a long talk with Abbasi, he thought.

△ △ △

Dawoud Abbasi stepped out of his Rolls Royce and examined the ruins of *Naqsh e-Rustam.* Also known as the Persian Crosses or the Necropolis, *Naqsh e-Rustam* was the final resting place of four ancient kings. Their tombs were carved into the rock in four identical cross shapes, which is where the local term Persian Crosses came from. In addition to the four tombs, the outer rock faces held seven relief carvings depicting seven of the Sassanid kings, the oldest of which dated back to 1000 BC.

Every time he looked upon the magnificent site, Dawoud felt an immense swelling of national pride. The Americans, in all their arrogance, believed they had a great history, but Dawoud knew the truth. History in the United States only went back to 1776—not even three hundred years. Even if you allowed for Columbus's voyage, America's Anglo-Saxon history still only stretched as far back as 1492, just over five hundred years.

Iran had been around for thousands and thousands of years. True, for much of that time it was known by other names, most notably Persia, but the rich heritage of his people could be traced back farther even than that of the ancient Greeks, to cities from 7000 to 8000 BC like Chogha Bonut and Susa, the latter of which still existed today. Despite the rest of the world's seeming refusal to acknowledge the facts, civilization began right here. In his beloved Iran.

The greatest nation on earth, he thought.

More than his sense of patriotism, Dawoud felt pride on a personal level every time he approached the tombs. The instrument of his greatest ambition was stored in a secret room that only he and a few others knew existed. Soon he would let loose a plague upon his enemies, just like the Jews' Jehovah. Ironically, a western industrialist had made it possible for Dawoud to conceive and execute his grand plan.

He could not believe his good fortune when his men stumbled upon an abandoned outpost in the Kavir Desert. The structure was clearly American in design, and all the signs and manuals had been printed in English. The two men inside, one of whom was already dead, were residents of the village of Hassi, just north of the site. Dawoud knew the village; he'd sent a group of soldiers there to recruit more men.

At first, he couldn't believe the Americans would be so brazen, but then when he realized what his men had uncovered, he knew it must be a sign from above. Many thousands of years ago, Persia was a great power, and the entire known world revolved around it. Now, the time had come to restore Iran to its former glory and strike a blow at the West at the same time. Using this fantastic monument to his people's heritage as a base of operations, Dawoud would begin his plan to bring the rest of the world to its knees.

His phone beeped twice, which was his assigned ring for text messages. He took out the phone and checked the screen, immediately pleased to see who it was from.

SUBJECT IS EN ROUTE. ETA: 2 HOURS.

Dawoud smiled and put the phone back in his pocket, not bothering to respond.

His son, lost to him for decades and presumed dead, was coming home.

He turned back to the Rolls Royce and poked his head into the door. Faiza sat in the cool air of the car's interior, reading a book about the Parthian Empire, which ruled over Iran from 238 BC–226 AD. Faiza seemed as fascinated by Iran's history as Dawoud, and the two would often have great discussions on the subject that lasted for hours. For that reason, he had not forbidden her to read, nor had he disciplined her too harshly for speaking her mind. He valued her input, and knew that if he was not careful he would lose that important aspect of their relationship. His other wives made up for her brashness, and were more than willing to pleasure him at his whim.

"Our son is on his way," he said. "He will be here in two hours."

"Here?" Faiza asked, waving her hand to indicate the area around the ruins.

"Where better?" Dawoud asked.

"The house in Tehran would have been suitable, I should think. It is certainly large enough to impress him."

"No, wife. You are missing the point. I will bring him here, to bask in the sight of this great monument to Iran's history, and impress upon him the glorious nature of our nation. He should begin to learn about his heritage as soon as possible."

"He was raised in America and joined the American military. Do you think he will abandon his previous life because of these ruins?" she asked.

"He is my son," Dawoud said. "Love of Iran is in his blood."

Faiza said nothing, merely nodding her head and returning to her book. Dawoud closed the door and pounded his hand on the roof of the car, which pulled away immediately. The driver was instructed to return Faiza to their home in Shiraz. Dawoud would join her later, if time permitted it. His wife did not know about his plan—she did not approve of his association with jihadists, and had been so bold as to tell him so on numerous occasions—but he would tell his son about them. The boy, now a man, would fall in love with the country, Dawoud felt it in his bones. And together they would usher in a new era of Iranian supremacy.

His smile grew larger as he turned and started walking toward the tomb of Xerxes I, which served as the entrance to a small network of rooms and chambers, accessible only from the rear of the tomb. The secrets contained in those dark corridors, both ancient and modern, were known only to a chosen few. His son would soon be one of those few. That feeling of pride returned. Not for his country this time, but for his blood.

His son was coming. He couldn't wait to meet him.

△ △ △

As soon as the door closed, Faiza put down her book. She hadn't been paying attention to it, anyway. It was merely a convenient method of keeping Dawoud from bothering her. She used her husband's interest in the history of Iran against him. Because of it, she had learned to read and write, and had much more freedom than the average Iranian woman. But it was all for show. She preferred reading material that wasn't so swamped with the "glorious history" of Iran. Not that she didn't love her country, but Dawoud's fascination with Iran's former greatness bordered on fanaticism, and she would rather read about things that affected the international community.

So, her son was coming home? She had hoped this day would never come, but once Dawoud heard from a source that his eldest heir wasn't dead, after all, he'd moved Heaven and Earth to find him. Faiza still recalled his reaction when he learned that his flesh and blood had joined the American Special Forces. It had taken the repairmen a week to patch the hole in the wall, and the imported cherry wood dining room table had to be thrown away. She had never seen him so angry, not even when the infant disappeared from his crib all those years ago.

She shuddered at the memory. He had been angry enough to kill someone that night, and she and the other wives had wisely stayed out of his way. Their son's identity had been discovered a year ago, and in the time since, her husband had turned his attention to ways to bring his estranged son home and make a patriotic Iranian of him. It was all he talked about now, and his anxiety and happiness grew exponentially the closer he came to achieving his goal. And now, it seemed, the day had come for his dream to be realized.

But how angry would Dawoud be when he learned the truth?

11.

Bishop's phone buzzed, and he looked at the screen. A text message from Deep Blue.

EXAMINATION OF ADDITIVE COMPLETE. VIRUS FATAL. INCUBATION PERIOD OF LESS THAN A MINUTE.

Bishop texted back:

SYMPTOMS?

After a few minutes, his phone buzzed again.

SIMILAR TO LSD: HALLUCINATIONS, VOMITING, ERRATIC AND VIOLENT BEHAVIOR. DEATH OCCURS IN ABOUT 24 HOURS. NO CURE. SENDING HELP.

Bishop typed his reply.

ALMOST TO TARGET NOW. WILL ADVISE UPON COMPLETION OF OBJECTIVE.

Thirty seconds later, his phone buzzed again.

GOOD. FRIENDLY AGENTS SHOULD BE USEFUL. BE CAREFUL.

Agents? As in more than one? Bishop looked at CJ, who was flying the plane and peering through the windshield. Was he supposed to have a partner? If so, what happened to him?

"Did you have a partner, CJ?" he asked.

CJ looked over, his customary smile gone. "Not anymore," he said.

Bishop took the hint and let it drop, but it still seemed strange. If CJ had recently lost a partner, then wouldn't Deep Blue have known about it? Deep Blue's text specifically said *agents*, plural, and he rarely made mistakes. Though it could have been a typo.

"There," CJ said, pointing out the right side window. "Our landing site."

Bishop looked, expecting to see an airport, but instead found himself staring at a rock face with four huge cross-shaped carvings cut from the stone. He recognized it from travel brochures as *Naqsh e-Rustam,* the burial site of four ancient kings. Why were they landing here? He had thought they were flying to Shiraz.

The answer came as a sharp pain in his throat. He whirled around in his seat, grabbing CJ's arm and yanking the needle out of his neck. He reached for his pistol with his other hand, but his arm seemed slow and heavy, and he only managed to get it around to the back of his waist. He could feel the grip of the pistol, but he couldn't close his fingers around it. Bishop's breathing increased as he began to wonder just what CJ had put in his system.

"Relax," CJ said. "It's not the Ergot B, if that's what you're thinking. If I wanted to kill you, I could have done it a thousand times already."

Bishop tried to reply, but could only manage a grunt. He focused his will on making words, and managed to croak out a slurred "What did you do to me?"

"It's just a hefty muscle relaxer," CJ continued. "Nonfatal, but you won't be feeling like yourself for a little while."

"Thought…Abbasi…"

"Oh, I'm taking you to Abbasi." CJ winked. "I just couldn't have you pulling your gun out and pointing it at him. I couldn't take the risk that you might actually shoot the guy. Then I'd never get paid."

"Son..of…a…"

"Terrorist?" CJ offered, laughing. "Nope. That's you, my friend. And he's very anxious to meet you."

Bishop tried to reply again, but he could no longer move his jaw. A few seconds later, he couldn't keep his eyes open.

Δ Δ Δ

The sleek black Sikorsky S-70 flew south toward Shiraz, with Massai and Ahmad seated in the back. The state-owned aircraft was specially modified for speed, and it sped across the sky at over 450 kp/h. They had contacted Shahid, their commander, the moment they drew close enough to Hassi to receive a signal on Massai's cell phone, and he had arranged for the S-70 to pick them up.

After boarding the plane, Massai had called Shahid back to confirm their pickup. To save time, he turned the phone on speaker, so everyone could hear, including the pilot.

"Not Shiraz," Shahid said. "*Naqsh e-Rustam.*"

"The tombs? Why?"

"That is where Abbasi is, and we have reason to believe that Joker will take Somers there to meet him. Our contact has hinted that something big is happening there, somewhere deep inside the stone itself."

"A contact, who remains anonymous," Massai replied. He had little use for such contacts.

"A contact that has not proven incorrect yet," Shahid reminded him. "It is not a request, Lieutenant Massai. It is an order. You and Ahmad will go to *Naqsh e-Rustam* right away."

"Yes, sir," Massai replied, and ended the call. He turned to Ahmad. "I guess we are going to *Naqsh e-Rustam*."

Ahmad nodded. "So I heard."

"'Somewhere deep inside the stone itself,'" Massai repeated. "How do we get inside the stone?"

"I do not know," Ahmad replied.

"I do," the pilot said.

Massai and Ahmad both turned to face the pilot, a middle-aged Iranian name Ishak.

"How do you know?" Massai asked.

"I was raised near there. I know all the local rumors and histories."

"And?"

"And there is a story about a panel near the rear of Xerxes I's tomb that, if pressed, will slide inward and admit the visitor to a secret network of caves and passages. According to legend, the ancient priests used these chambers to keep vigil over the dead kings to ensure they did not rise again."

"Have you ever seen this panel?" Ahmad asked.

"No," Ishak said.

"Then how do you know it is there?" Massai asked.

"I do not," Ishak admitted.

Massai looked at Ahmad, waiting for his friend to tell him that Allah would provide, but Ahmad merely shrugged his shoulders.

"We have nothing else to try." Ahmad said. "Shahid has ordered us to *Naqsh e-Rustam*."

"Massai nodded. "And so that is where we will go."

"If there is an entrance into the stone," Ahmad said, "we will find it when we get there."

12.

Dawoud rose from his seat as CJ entered the room, followed by two men carrying a stretcher between them. On the stretcher lay his son, unconscious.

"What happened?" Dawoud asked.

"He grew suspicious," CJ answered. "Someone must have leaked our information."

Faiza. It had to be. Only she would be so bold as to go against him in this. He had thought she didn't know about his plans, but perhaps he was mistaken.

"It does not matter," Dawoud said. "I have my son and the Ergot-B. Everything is moving along as planned."

He walked over to the stretcher and took his first look as his son and heir, who had spent his entire life ignorant of his heritage. But as soon as he saw the man's face, he knew something was wrong. It took a moment for the thought to come full circle, but then he realized the truth. He had been lied to for decades.

"This man," Dawoud said through clenched teeth, "is not my son."

"What?" CJ asked. "Sure he is. That's what Faiza told me."

"Faiza lied!" Dawoud's face grew bright red, and the two men holding the stretcher flinched. "She has been lying for decades. Look at this man's nose, his cheekbones, his lips. He is not my son."

CJ looked at Bishop. After a moment, he looked back to Dawoud. "I think you're right."

"I know I am right."

"Then whose son is he?" CJ asked.

Dawoud's vision clouded, and his breathing and heart rate both sped up. His fists clenched at his side. He knew who the father was, but he would not share that information with CJ. The traitorous Delta operative didn't have need to know the whole story, but Dawoud had seen those same features on a man he had known and trusted for many years. He wasn't sure which betrayal hurt more, his or Faiza's.

Either way, now he would have to kill them both, as well as this bastard in front of him.

△ △ △

In the back of the Rolls Royce, Faiza Abbasi shut off her cell phone and put it into her pocket. Weeks ago, she had sent information to an American soldier in Iran, hoping he would help her leave the country and reunite her with her son in exchange for years of information about her husband's activities, which she had carefully and thoroughly catalogued for decades. But instead of helping her, he had taken the information of Erik's whereabouts to her husband and sold it to him. Now that same man had her son, and was bringing him to Dawoud.

She should have left things as they were. If not for her weakness, Erik would still be in the United States, instead of flying through Iran on his way to his death.

Many years ago, Faiza had been given to Dawoud by her father as a bride in exchange for a lucrative business deal. She did not love Dawoud, and never had. He was an ambitious, aggressive man who was seldom home. Even when he was home, he treated Faiza as little more than a sex toy, only coming to her when he required a release. She came to despise his touch, but as a woman in Iran, she had no right to deny him. He came into her rooms often enough, but much to her dismay, they never had any children. She longed for a baby to care for, hoping that a child would soften her husband and provide her with someone to love. But no matter how many times they tried, no baby landed in her belly.

Soon enough he tired of her and brought in a new wife, and then another and another. She hoped she would be able to make friends among them, but they were jealous of her standing as Dawoud's first wife, and wanted nothing to do with her. Miserable and lonely, she spent her days walking through the gardens, longing to break free of her stylish prison. It became so bad that she had even contemplated ending her own life.

But all that changed when Dawoud hired a new driver for her.

Anwar was strong, handsome and kind. He treated her well and respected her words, which no one had ever done before. At first, she thought his courtesy was the result of her husband's status, but soon she realized that Anwar did not look at Dawoud's other wives the way he looked at her. One day, as he helped her to load some packages into the car, his hand brushed against hers and she looked up at his face. In that moment, she realized that he loved her.

In all Faiza's life, no man had ever looked at her the way Anwar did. Not her father, who cared more about what his beautiful daughter could bring him, nor her brothers, to whom she was just another female in the house, and certainly not her husband, who used her when he needed her and then left her alone; no man, she realized, had ever loved her.

Their affair was short but magnificent. Anwar's passion sizzled, and his touch seared her flesh every time they met. They knew they could both be killed for their transgression, but neither cared. For her, life without him felt like death, and she would not give him up. Not even to save her life. But then, as so often seemed to happen, things changed suddenly.

Faiza became pregnant.

Now she had more to worry about than just her desires. Once the child was born, Dawoud would have known it was not his, and he would have killed her and the baby, as well. She ended her affair with Anwar, telling him it was wrong and they should be ashamed. He had stayed on as her driver, unwilling to give up on her, but eventually he moved on and found another love. She never told him about the baby, though she thought he suspected. And even now, he sat in the driver's seat of the Rolls Royce, taking her back to her home in Shiraz.

After ending the affair, she sought her husband's bed for the first time in years. Dawoud was so pleased by her aggressiveness that he began seeking her company again and again, and soon the two were spending almost every night in each other's arms.

When she told him she was pregnant, his smile took up half his face.

Of course, she knew the math would not work. But she gambled that her husband would be out of town when her time came, and she was right. She had gone into labor while he was away in Saudi Arabia, believing she still had another month to go before delivery. By the time he was able to get back, the baby was gone.

He raised a tremendous row, threatening to bring legal and illegal retribution to everyone in the hospital, but in the end, it changed nothing. The Abbasi son was gone, and no one seemed able to find him. She played her part well, acting outraged and despondent. It was not difficult to pretend she was grief-stricken; sending her son away was the hardest thing she had ever done, but it was best. He would live, and so would she.

But now her secret would be revealed, and her son would pay the price. Dawoud was an ambitious man, and he was intelligent. It would not take him long to realize that Erik Somers was not his son. And then he would kill Erik, her and Anwar, as well.

But she still had one more card to play, and she had just played it.

She hoped it would be enough.

13.

When Bishop awoke, he was strapped to a chair inside a stone chamber. Next to him on his right was a row of large metal tanks, at least a dozen of them, each labeled in Persian: DANGER. The tanks also had the biohazard symbol stenciled on the side. Bishop had no trouble imaging what the tanks contained. And from the sheer quantity of fluid the tanks could hold, it appeared Dawoud meant to poison the entire world.

Across the room, on a small metal table, sat Bishop's things. His Sig Sauer pistol, extra clips, knife and backpack. The bottle of water was just visible under the flap, but the knife would have been the most useful. The straps felt like thick plastic zip ties—the kind used by police to secure prisoners—but he couldn't see them. Most likely they would be too strong to snap. CJ would have seen to that.

He tried anyway, but he was too weak. All he managed to do was make enough noise to draw attention.

"He's awake," came a familiar voice from his left. Bishop turned to see CJ standing over him, the Beretta in hand.

"You were part of it," Bishop said. "You were with the jihadists in Hassi."

CJ nodded. "Took you long enough."

"You set the trap," Bishop said.

CJ smiled. "Good thing you kept me from opening it quickly.

Bishop frowned. CJ's rush to open the hatch had been a ruse, as was his feigned surprise that caused him to fall off the edge.

"Though I was kind of worried you'd take the shot full on. How's the arm, by the way?"

"Fuck off," Bishop said.

"Come on, B, don't be like that. I just wanted to reunite you with your folks."

"You just wanted to get paid."

"Fair enough." CJ winked.

The man from the photo, Dawoud Abbasi, stepped around CJ and stood in front of Bishop, staring down at him. "You are not my son," the man said.

"Best news I've heard all day," Bishop retorted.

CJ chuckled, but Dawoud silenced him with a glare.

"Apologies, Dawoud," CJ said. "He caught me off guard with that one."

Dawoud nodded and then turned back to Bishop. "You are the bastard son of my wife and her driver. His features are stamped all over your face."

Bishop said nothing, keeping his face neutral and calm, but inside, he felt a surge of relief that he was not, in fact, related to a terrorist leader.

"What are you going to do to him?" CJ asked.

Dawoud reached over to the small table and picked up the Sig Sauer pistol. He checked the clip, then slid it home and pulled back the slide. "I should think that would be obvious," he replied.

"Sorry, B," CJ said. "I never intended for you to get killed. You were supposed to be his son."

Bishop just glared up at him.

"That's right," Dawoud said. "He was supposed to be my son." Without another word, Dawoud whirled around, put the pistol to CJ's head, and pulled the trigger. The sound inside the stone chamber was deafening, and Bishop winced in spite of himself. The side of CJ's head exploded in a burst of red as blood and bits of brain and bone flew outward from the exit wound. As the body tumbled to the floor, Bishop couldn't help but notice that CJ's ever-present smile was forever replaced by a look of surprise and fear.

"I don't like it when people fail me," Dawoud offered by way of explanation. "I paid him a great deal of money to bring my son to me, and instead he brought you."

Bishop looked up, knowing he was next and wanting to meet his fate head on. To his surprise, Dawoud turned away from him and set the pistol on the table. When he looked back at Bishop, his features hardened.

"I have sent men after my wife and your father," he said. "They will bring them here soon enough. I want her to watch as I kill the two of you."

△ △ △

Massai couldn't believe his eyes when he read the text message on his phone.

They were still in the Sikorsky, but were nearing their destination. He and Ahmad had been going over every piece of information they could get on the tomb of Xerxes I, hoping to find a clue about how to get inside the *Naqsh e-Rustam.* They hadn't found anything, and were beginning to worry that they might not be able to get inside.

Then he'd received the text.

After reading it, he looked up from his mobile device. "I know how to get in," he said.

"How?" Ahmad asked.

Massai showed him the text.

Ahmad smiled. "See? Allah will—"

"Provide," Massai finished. He turned to Ishak. "How long until we reach the site?"

"Twenty minutes," Ishak replied.

Massai put the phone back in his pocket and began to check his pistol, wanting to make sure it was fully loaded. Twenty minutes, and now they knew how to get inside the facility. He took a deep breath, said a rare prayer and waited. His muscles itched in anticipation, but he forced himself to stay still. His arms and legs would get a workout soon enough.

14.

The sound of a metal door clanging against stone brought Bishop to attention. He couldn't see the door, but he heard the voices. One of them, a woman's voice, pleaded for mercy.

"Please do not do this," she screamed. Her cries ended with the sound of a slap.

"Bring them," Dawoud said.

In a few seconds, two people were dragged in front of Bishop's chair—a man and a woman; both looked as though they'd been roughed up by their captors. He recognized the tear-streaked face of the woman, having seen it in the photo. The man with her must be his real father. This was not at all how he envisioned meeting them.

"Erik!" the woman cried. "Erik, please forgive me."

Bishop would have liked to forgive her, but at that moment, he was too angry. The pressure in his head had been building up ever since Dawoud had told him the truth, and by the time his biological parents were brought in front of him, all he could see was a wall of red. At the center of that wall stood Dawoud Abbasi, his pistol loaded and pointed right at Bishop's head.

"Tell *your* son goodbye," Dawoud said.

"No!" Faiza cried. "No, please, Dawoud. Please!" She reached over to clutch at his leg, but he kicked her away.

"Tell him goodbye, Faiza!" Dawoud's face was bright red, his jaw clenched and tense. "Tell him goodbye or I will kill him slow."

Faiza squeezed her eyes shut and shook her head. Bishop understood. She couldn't do it.

"Goodbye," Bishop said for her.

Movement to the side caught his eye as the man, his father, jerked free from his captors and launched himself at Dawoud. Voices filled the chamber as four men swore in Persian. Dawoud had just enough time to turn and fire before both of them fell into a heap on the floor.

"Anwar!" Faiza screamed.

Bishop watched as the limp body of his biological father fell to the ground. He saw the splotch of blood begin to pool under the man's chest, and he watched as Dawoud struggled to push the dead weight off of him. As he struggled, Bishop saw Dawoud's face, glaring at him.

Bishop's vision narrowed with a surge of adrenaline. He could see nothing except the body of his father and the face of the man who murdered him. Nothing else in the room registered. He tried to stand, but something held him back. In his state, he could not tell what it was, so he pushed against it. Bishop's muscles bulged as he struggled to move forward.

Seeing the life drain from his father's body—a man he would now never get a chance to know—focused Bishop's rage. He strained tighter against his bonds. Had he still been able to regenerate his body, he would yank until the flesh peeled from his bone. The sting of fresh wounds on his wrists and the trickle of warm blood over his palms told him he was about to do just that. But he banked on his muscles and bones being strong than plastic, and pulled harder. His wounds might not heal in an instant, but they would not kill him.

He would heal in time.

His father would not.

Bishop gave a quick, hard tug, and the plastic relented to his brute strength. With the resistance gone, Bishop stumbled forward, off balance. Free of his restraints, he saw Dawoud sitting up, reaching for his pistol, which lay on the floor next to him. Bishop got there first, however, and kicked the gun across the room. Then he reached down, grabbed Dawoud by his shirt collar and picked him up. He didn't even notice the weight.

In his mind, all he saw was a threat, and Bishop's instincts told him what to do next. He reached his hand around Dawoud's throat and started to squeeze. The muscles in his massive arms bulged as his grip tightened, and Dawoud sputtered and cursed as he tried to claw at Bishop's forearms. Soon the terrorist's head turned an ugly shade of purple.

A loud crack sounded through the room, and at first Bishop thought he had broken Dawoud's neck, but then the pain in his shoulder registered and his left arm dropped from Dawoud's throat. It took him a moment to realize he'd been shot. His field of vision opened up, and he was able to see everything clearly. His mother squatted next to the chair he'd been strapped to, a small knife in her hand. As strong as Bishop was, he hadn't been the one to break the plastic bonds. It had been his Faiza's—his mother's—blade. He would have to thank her. Later. His current concerns were Dawoud's men, who pointed their pistols at him and continued shooting.

Amateurs, Bishop thought. *They could have killed Dawoud.* That the men had poor aim was a good thing. But their inexperience also made them dangerously unpredictable.

He released Dawoud and dropped to the floor just as a round buzzed by his head. He rolled to the side and hid behind one of the tanks just in time to avoid another bullet as it passed within an inch of his shoulder.

From behind the tank, he saw that Faiza had gone. She must have used the distraction to escape. The only people left in the room were Dawoud and a pair of his henchmen. Dawoud was getting to his feet while the two men fired at Bishop. They weren't very good with their pistols, but at this range, they didn't have to be. If not for his instincts, Bishop would be full of holes.

"No," Dawoud screamed, "You'll release the Ergot-B!" But it was too late. The man on the right fired a shot that penetrated one of the tanks, and ergot-contaminated water began to spray into the room. "You fools! The ergot can soak through the skin!" he turned to run, and Bishop needed no further urging. He leapt out from behind the tank and ran after Dawoud.

He only made it halfway across the room when a heavy weight crashed into him from behind and he tumbled to the floor, landing on his injured shoulder a few feet from the growing puddle of poisoned water. Bishop winced in pain, and the guard who had tackled him saw an advantage. He pressed his knee into the back of Bishop's shoulder, sending waves of pain through him. For a moment, Bishop's vision blurred, and then he heard the unmistakable click of a pistol slide behind his head.

The pain vanished, and Bishop rolled to the side just as the shot went off. The bullet tore a chunk of stone from the floor just to the left of Bishops head, sending rock fragments everywhere. A few chips of stone flew into his face, stinging but doing little damage.

The guard who'd been sitting on his back lost his balance and fell over into the spreading puddle of ergot-contaminated water. The other guard stood over Bishop, pistol in hand, as he adjusted his aim. No time to do anything fancy. Bishop launched a kick to the man's groin that lifted him off the floor.

The man grunted in pain as he fell to the stone, just missing the puddle that was even now lapping at Bishop's shoes. His pistol clattered away, coming to a stop underneath a bank of computer equipment.

With a manic shriek, the guard who'd fallen in the puddle of ergot shot to his feet. He craned his head back and forth, looking at the room with wide, confused eyes, as though he'd just woken up from a nightmare. Then his eyes locked on Bishop. The man's fingers curled. He was clearly mad, and about to attack, but it wasn't the man's physical prowess that gave Bishop pause, it was the fact that the man was dripping with Ergot-B.

If the man landed a punch, or even managed to scratch Bishop, he would descend into madness.

"Not again," Bishop said. "Never again!"

The man charged.

Bishop sidestepped at the last moment and delivered a spinning kick to the man's back, sending him spilling into the stone wall. The impact would have made any rational man think twice about continuing the fight, but this man couldn't be talked down from his ergot-induced mania. He shoved himself up and charged again.

This time, Bishop didn't sidestep. He needed to end this fight.

Permanently.

He stepped back, into the pool of Ergot-B, protected from its effect by the thick rubber soles of his boots. As the man closed the distance between them, Bishop pushed himself up between two of the big tanks and kicked out with the steel-toed tip of his boot. There was a crack, and he felt the man's head cave a little beneath the force of the kick. The man crumpled like God had reached down and yanked his power cord from the wall.

Bishop lowered himself carefully and stepped out of the puddle, making a mental note to be very careful when he took off his boots. The other man stirred, pushing himself up. Bishop stopped, smashed his sledgehammer fist into the man's head, knocking him out, and then ran toward the exit. Along the way, he saw his pistol lying on the stone floor, miraculously untouched by the ergot water. He reached down to pick it up.

He took off down the hall after Dawoud, having no clear idea where he was going. He couldn't let the man get away, though. The information in the man's head was too valuable. Abbasi was a terrorist leader, with knowledge of perhaps hundreds of active cells and their locations, possibly even their planned attacks. If he could bring him in, there was no telling how much they could learn from him. Not to mention it would give him a large amount of satisfaction to give the man a few good punches to the gut.

He caught a glimpse of Dawoud up ahead and sped up, dodging aside as a bullet pinged off the stone to his right. Dawoud fired two more shots, and Bishop returned fire. Then he turned the corner and ran up a hallway, catching sight of Dawoud again as the man ran through a doorway.

Bishop followed as fast as he could, but the pain in his shoulder and the loss of blood combined with the aftereffects of the drugs to slow him down. He wheezed and coughed, but kept running, even after he lost sight of Dawoud again. After a few minutes, his steps slowed. The passages of *Naqsh e-Rustam* were larger and more complex than he would have thought. He tried to remember where he was through the growing fog in his brain. Had he taken a right or a left back there? He couldn't remember. He was completely turned around. Still, he kept going.

Dawoud could not escape. He would not allow it.

Bishop ran around a corner and slammed right into a person on the other side. Dawoud! He raised his pistol to fire, but it was knocked aside. He staggered back and raised his fists, ready to brawl with Dawoud if he needed to.

"Be calm, Somers," a voice said. "We are here to help."

Bishop took a deep breath and forced himself to calm down. Through a haze of pain and exhaustion, the person's face came into focus. He looked familiar, but Bishop couldn't quite place him. The man reached into his pocket and Bishop tensed, but he only pulled out a badge. "My name is Massai," the man said. "Iranian Special Forces."

Behind Massai, Bishop saw a man holding on to a squirming, cursing Dawoud Abbasi.

"That's Ahmad," Massai said. "We were supposed to meet you at the airport, but you got into a taxi and left with the Joker."

Of course. The two men from Imam Khomeini. That's where he knew them from. They must be the men that Deep Blue had sent. And they were never trying to kill *him*. Just Joker.

"You guys are Special Forces?" Bishop asked, wheezing.

Massai nodded.

Bishop sat down, breathing long and loud. "You guys suck," he said.

15.

Dawoud couldn't believe it as he was led back through the facility. The two Iranian agents had captured him right as he was leaving the *Naqsh e-Rustam*. How had they known how to get inside?

Faiza, it had to be her. She must have known more than she allowed him to believe.

A flood of Iranian soldiers poured into the facility, shooting first and not bothering with questions. Of course now that he had been exposed, the government would move fast to make it seem as though they had no idea what was going on here. They would pretend Dawoud had acted alone, and without the cooperation of the Iranian government. No one would believe them, of course, but it wouldn't matter. The UN would never investigate for fear of insulting the current regime.

At least they fear us enough for that, he thought, a bitter smile on his lips.

Of more concern was the United States. Somers would insist on taking Dawoud back to America to face trial, but Dawoud knew the truth. There would be no trial if he went to America. There would only be a cell, some ratty clothing, and a handful of specialists who knew how to extract information from reluctant prisoners.

He regretted the loss of his pistol. It had run out of ammunition during his failed escape and he'd tossed it away. He should have saved one last round just in case. If he'd had it in his possession when Massai corralled him, he could have at least put a bullet in his own head and died with honor. Dawoud knew his worth. He knew his strengths and weaknesses, but he also knew how interrogations worked. He'd seen plenty of them firsthand, even participated in a few. One thing he knew for certain: sooner or later, *everyone* talked. He would be no different.

He was led into the room with the large tanks. The spilled ergot water had been hosed away, and the bodies lined up along the wall. Faiza was there, as well as her son. She was dressed like a Westerner, her *habib* nowhere to be seen and her face bare for every man in the room to see. Her face was streaked with tears, but Erik's simmered with anger. The two stood far apart, and he felt a small bit of satisfaction knowing that her betrayal had not helped her to reunite with her son. The man seemed to want nothing to do with her. As well he might, given the circumstances. She had lied to every one of them.

Still, she would have the last laugh as she watched the American dogs drag him away in chains. The thought bothered him even more than the idea of being arrested. That she should get to watch him in his disgrace seemed like the ultimate insult. She deserved to die for her infidelity and her lies, yet there she stood, her attention split between her bastard of a son and her husband. She would be ushered out of the country to live the American lifestyle she'd always wanted, while he would scream for mercy in a cell somewhere. It wasn't fair.

How he longed for the pistol now. Death would be far better than this humiliation. But as he looked around, he saw one last chance for redemption.

And he meant to take it.

△ △ △

Bishop stood looking down at the body of Anwar Muaddah, driver for Dawoud Abbasi and also his biological father. His face looked familiar to Bishop, and he realized it was because he'd seen those same features every day for his entire life. He resembled the dead man so much that it was no wonder Dawoud knew the truth right away.

He turned to look at his mother, Faiza Abbasi, who stood about ten feet away with a blanket wrapped around her shoulders. Bishop's own shoulder had been cleaned and bandaged, and his left arm hung in a sling. The woman in front of him looked exactly like the picture. Pretty, in an older woman sort of way. Her dark hair streaked with gray. The only real difference was her outfit.

Instead of her black *habib,* Bishop noticed, Faiza was dressed in blue jeans, sneakers and a dark blouse with the top button undone. Quite daring for a conservative Muslin town like Shiraz. And then the reason came to him.

"You were leaving," he said from across the room. "Weren't you?"

She nodded, tears spilling onto her cheeks. "I know Shahid Millik, the Commander of Iran's Special Forces. I've been sending him information for months. After I sent him the text message explaining how to get inside the *Naqsh e-Rustam,* I called Anwar. His wife died several years ago, and we have been planning to leave the country for months. With everything that was happening, today seemed like a good day to do it."

"Adulteress!" came the shout from behind his back. Bishop turned to see Dawoud struggling to get free of the agent holding him. The agent slipped on the wet floor, and Dawoud took advantage of the moment to sweep his leg out from under him.

Before anyone in the room could draw a pistol, Dawoud's hand struck out for Bishop's backpack.

The alarms in Bishop's head started to fire. There was a knife in there! He moved out of instinct to push his mother out of harm's way, certain that she would be the target. But instead of the knife, Dawoud pulled out the water bottle Bishop had taken from the Manifold site. The bright yellow biohazard symbol gleamed in the light from the room's lamps.

"Stop him," Bishop shouted, knowing what Dawoud meant to do.

Dawoud unscrewed the cap and brought the bottle to his mouth. Before Massai tackled him, he managed to take several swallows of the infected water.

The effect was immediate. Dawoud started screaming and punching at Massai, shoving him upward like he was a toy. He sprang to his feet. He looked around, his eyes wild, and reached into the backpack for the knife. Bishop recalled the words of Deep Blue's text.

NO CURE.

Dawoud must have known that.

The terrorist leader looked around the room, and then his eyes settled on Faiza. He flashed a lopsided grin, drooling from the corner of his mouth, and launched himself at her before anyone in the room had time to react. His fingers curled around the handle of the KA-BAR as he brought it up for a strike. His garbled words were unintelligible, but his intent was clear.

Faiza screamed.

Bishop kicked the man square in the chest, wanting to distance him and his mother from the man's body in case Dawoud had spilled any of the Ergot-B on himself. A series of sharp cracks tore through the air and Bishop felt the man's ribcage cave. Then the force of the kick sent the man flying backwards.

As he sailed through the air, Bishop pulled his Sig and fired a single shot. The round entered Dawoud's head on the left and exited on the right, spraying blood and gore around the room. The body fell twitching to the floor, blood pooling out.

Faiza's eyes rolled into her head, then her limp body crumpled to the ground like a sack of laundry. Bishop reached out just in time to keep her head from banging into the floor.

He picked her up as the rest of the room exploded into chaos. Iranian Special Forces agents scrambled through the place, swearing and yelling in Persian. Bishop ignored them and lifted his prone mother over his good shoulder. She stirred as he carried her out of the room, ignoring the pain in his shoulder. Her eyes opened, and she smiled weakly. She brought her hand up to brush against his stubbly cheek.

"Erik?" she said. "Can you forgive me?"

"Shhh," he replied. "You're safe now, mother."

She smiled and put her head on his chest.

He'd found his mother, and was proud of what she'd done—and where he'd come from.

For the first time in his life, Erik Somers, callsign: Bishop, felt no anger at all.

EPILOGUE

Tehran, two days later.

Bishop walked into the restaurant and looked around. He spotted her right away, sitting in a corner booth. She was back to wearing her *habib,* which would be appropriate since she had not yet left Iran. The two Iranian guards behind her nodded to him as he approached. Since Dawoud's death, the terrorist's colleagues had made numerous attempts to silence anyone in Dawoud's family who might know too much. So far, several of his wives had been killed, but with the help of the Iranian military, Faiza was smuggled out of Shiraz and into Tehran, where it would be easier for her to vanish. Soon she would be able to come to the States, and she could drop the *habib* in favor of blue jeans again.

She watched him approach. Her face still lined with grief. He had not been permitted to see her after the mess in *Naqsh e-Rustam.* The Iranian government's position was that nothing unusual had occurred, and any rumors to the contrary were just that: rumors. The site had been closed for "renovations," which is where the government claimed the rumors got their start.

But now, finally, the government had allowed the two to meet. They chose a public place, where their conversation could be monitored and recorded. Bishop didn't care. He'd expected no less. Besides, he doubted the Iranian government would be interested in their conversation, anyway.

As he sat down, a million questions ran through his mind. Questions about his grandparents, about Anwar, about her life as a terrorist's wife. He wanted to know what it was like for her all those years, not knowing where he was or what he was doing. He had a feeling he already knew why she gave him up, but he would ask her that, too.

In addition, he could see on her face that she had questions for him, as well. He hoped he could answer all of them.

"Hello, Mother," he said.

"Hello, Erik," she replied.

"I think we should talk," he said.

She smiled, which did nothing to erase the sadness in her face. "Yes, we should."

ABOUT THE AUTHORS

JEREMY ROBINSON is the author of eleven novels including PULSE, INSTINCT, and THRESHOLD the first three books in his exciting Jack Sigler series. His novels have been translated into nine languages. He lives in New Hampshire with his wife and three children.

Visit him on the web, here: www.jeremyrobinsononline.com

DAVID MCAFEE is the author of the 2010 bestselling horror novel, *33 A.D.*, as well as several other horror titles currently available on Amazon Kindle and elsewhere. He is currently working on the third book in his *Bachiyr* series. He lives in Tennessee with his wife, daughter, and infant son.

Visit him on the web, here: mcafeeland.wordpress.com

ALSO IN 2011

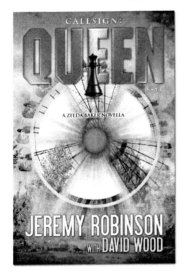

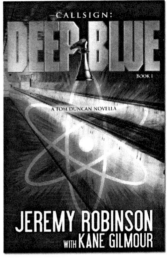

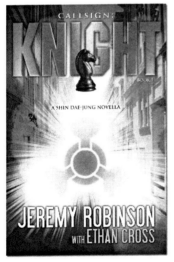

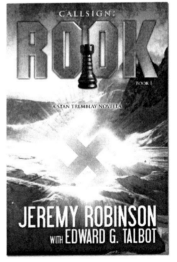

CPSIA information can be obtained at www.ICGtesting.com
Printed in the USA
LVOW120637191211

260055LV00005B/1/P